OrangeBooks Publication

1st Floor, Rajhans Arcade, Mall Road, Kohka, Bhilai, Chhattisgarh 490020

Website: **www.orangebooks.in**

First Edition, 2025

ISBN: 978-93-6554-502-9

Price: Rs. 325.00

Printed in India

THE LIBRARY OF FORGOTTEN BOOKS

SOUMIK CHATTERJEE

OrangeBooks Publication
www.orangebooks.in

Preface

This story began on a winter night with a simple request:

"Baba, will you write a story for me?"

That was Kurchi, my daughter—curious, creative, and full of wonder. She and her two closest friends have been inseparable since they were small. At school, everyone knows them as the Three Musketeers. They tell stories, solve problems together, and dream out loud with the kind of magic only childhood friendship can conjure.

For days, I struggled to find the right story to tell them. Then something changed. One day, I heard Kurchi praised for her singing. Soon after, her friend was celebrated for her academic brilliance. And in those moments, a world began to form—one where music opened enchanted books, riddles unlocked ancient doors, and memory became the most powerful kind of magic.

Kurchi, Ghurni, and Meghna were born not just from imagination, but from love—from the quiet strength of children who support one another, each bringing their own light into the world.

This book is for them—and for every child who believes in the power of stories, the importance of friendship, and the quiet courage it takes to remember when the world starts to forget.

Thank you for joining them on this adventure.

Dedication

For my daughter and her two dearest friends—

the true spark behind this story.

Index

Chapter 1
Rooftop Evenings

The sun was just beginning to dip below the horizon, casting a soft orange glow across the small suburban town of Sundargram. The late afternoon breeze rustled the leaves of the tall mango tree growing in the corner of the veranda. It was the perfect time for Kurchi, Ghurni, and Meghna to meet, as they did every day after school.

Kurchi's rooftop room was their sanctuary, a place where they could talk freely, solve puzzles, and daydream about adventures. It wasn't a large room, but it had everything they needed—a couple of worn-out armchairs, shelves filled with old, dusty books, and windows that overlooked the narrow lanes and the sloping rooftops of Sundargram.

Kurchi's father, a househusband, had designed the room himself. He was always tinkering with new ideas, filling the shelves with quirky knick-knacks and books that he collected from his travels. Some were ancient texts on history and mythology, others about mathematics, and some were whimsical tales of magical realms. It was a treasure trove of knowledge, and the girls often spent hours reading and discussing the strange stories or solving the puzzles Kurchi's father often left lying around.

Today was no different. As Kurchi opened the heavy wooden door that led to the rooftop room, she felt the familiar sense of calm settle over her. The room smelled of old paper and fresh jasmine from the flowers growing in the window box.

Ghurni and Meghna were already there, sitting cross-legged on the floor, their schoolbags tossed to one side. Ghurni was the first to greet Kurchi, her face lighting up with excitement.

"Kurchi, you won't believe what happened in class today! Mrs. Gupta couldn't solve the logic puzzle I gave her!" Ghurni giggled, her eyes sparkling with mischief. "I told her it was too easy for a teacher."

Kurchi smiled warmly as she dropped her schoolbag on the nearby chair. "You always know how to make school interesting, Ghurni. I don't think I could ever beat you at a logic game."

Meghna, ever the quiet one, looked up from the corner of the room where she was sitting by the small window, her attention drawn to the busy street below. She wasn't as vocal as Ghurni, but when she spoke, her words carried weight. "I won the treasure hunt again," she said, her voice low but steady. "Nobody could figure out the clues, but I cracked them all. It's not as fun anymore when you know you're going to win."

Kurchi chuckled, "You're humble, Meghna. That's why we love having you around."

Meghna gave a small smile, then turned back to the window, lost in her thoughts. It was clear that Meghna enjoyed the company of her friends, but she often seemed like she was observing the world around her with a deeper curiosity than most people.

"So, what are we doing today?" Ghurni asked, eager for their usual adventure.

Kurchi looked around the room, her mind already wandering to the many possibilities. Her father had once told her that every room in their house had a story to tell, if only one was willing to listen carefully enough. Her father loved stories, especially old ones, and often invited the girls to listen to his tales of faraway places and magical creatures. But today was different.

"Well, I was thinking we could try one of the puzzles my father left on the shelf," Kurchi said, her voice filled with excitement. "You know, the one about the hidden treasure? I'm sure it's not as easy as it looks."

Meghna raised an eyebrow, intrigued. "You mean that old puzzle he got from the antique shop last week?"

Ghurni nodded. "I think I've seen that one before. It looks impossible."

"Exactly," Kurchi replied, her eyes gleaming. "That's why I'm sure we can solve it. We're the best team for the job."

They all settled down on the floor, facing the shelf that was home to numerous books and puzzles. Kurchi's father had a collection of rare artifacts—odd trinkets, ancient maps, and mysterious-looking objects—and it was often these objects that served as the foundation for their daily adventures.

After rummaging through the stack of books, Kurchi found a small wooden box at the back. It was intricately carved, with swirling patterns that seemed to dance in the dim light. She handed it over to Ghurni, who was always the one to figure out how to open things that were locked or tricky to solve.

"This one looks like it's been around for ages," Ghurni said, running her fingers along the carvings. "Let me see if I can crack it."

Kurchi leaned back against the armchair, watching her friend work. She loved moments like this—when everything felt calm and their only task was to solve a puzzle together.

Meghna, meanwhile, was staring out the window, her thoughts clearly elsewhere. She wasn't as interested in puzzles as the others. She preferred to observe the world, piecing together patterns from what she saw around her. It wasn't uncommon for Meghna to notice something the others didn't.

Ghurni fiddled with the box for a few more minutes before she finally sighed in frustration. "I can't figure it out. This one's tough."

Meghna stood up, moved to the shelf, and picked up a small silver trinket that Kurchi's father had once explained was an old compass. As soon as Meghna touched it, the air in the room seemed to change, just slightly—but enough for Kurchi to notice.

"What's that?" Kurchi asked, curious.

"I don't know," Meghna said softly. "It just felt... important."

Suddenly, there was a sharp knock on the door. Kurchi's father, who had been working in the kitchen, stepped in with a tray of steaming cups of chai and a plate of freshly made samosas. "I thought you might be hungry by now," he said with a smile, setting the tray down in front of the girls. "Kurchi, don't forget to take a break every now and then. All that puzzling isn't good for your mind."

Kurchi smiled up at him. "Thanks, Papa."

Her father was an unusual man—always tinkering with things, lost in his own thoughts. But he had a way of making every day feel special, especially when he told stories. Kurchi often wondered how her father knew so much about the world, about far-off places and hidden truths. He had a gift for making even the most ordinary things seem extraordinary.

As they ate their snacks, her father began telling them one of his usual stories. "Did I ever tell you about the lost library?" he began. "It was said to contain the most powerful knowledge in the world, hidden away from those who might misuse it…"

Kurchi, Ghurni, and Meghna listened intently, their eyes wide with wonder as her father continued. The story was one they had heard before, but it never lost its charm. It was about a group of children, much like them, who had discovered a hidden world of knowledge—one filled with books that held secrets no one else could understand.

"The thing about that library," her father said, his eyes glinting with mystery, "was that it wasn't just any library. It was protected by a riddle, and only those with the right abilities could find it."

Kurchi felt a shiver run down her spine. Her father's stories always felt like more than just stories—they felt like hints, like the beginning of something important. She looked at Ghurni and Meghna, who both seemed equally intrigued.

Her father leaned in closer, lowering his voice. "But the real secret is that the library isn't just about knowledge.

It's about power. The kind of power that can change the world."

For a moment, the room was silent. The weight of his words hung in the air. Kurchi felt something stir inside her—a curiosity that had always been there but was now beginning to grow stronger.

Ghurni broke the silence. "How do you find it, Uncle?"

Her father smiled, as if he'd been waiting for that question. "Ah, that's the tricky part. The library doesn't reveal itself to just anyone. You have to be chosen." He stood up and began clearing away the dishes, his voice returning to its usual playful tone. "But don't worry about that for now. It's just a story, after all."

Chapter 2
The Book in the Attic

The sky had turned to a dusky shade of rose, and the rooftop room glowed in the warm light of evening. Kurchi, Ghurni, and Meghna were curled up in their usual spots, half-talking, half-lost in thought. The jasmine from the window box still scented the air, and Kurchi's father's voice lingered in their minds from the story he'd just told—about a lost library hidden behind riddles and music.

"That was one of his best," Ghurni said, stretching out with a satisfied sigh. "Do you think he makes them all up?"

Kurchi shook her head. "I don't think so. He knows too much. It's like he's... remembering."

Meghna had been quietly staring at the wooden shelf lined with trinkets and puzzles. "That story," she said softly, "felt different. Like it was meant for us."

There was a pause. Then Kurchi sat up, her eyes thoughtful. "Have either of you ever been to the attic?"

Both girls looked at her.

"No," said Ghurni. "I thought it was locked."

Kurchi smiled slowly. "It's not. Papa always said it's just full of old stuff, and a bit dusty. But... he also once said it holds 'forgotten treasures.' I think he was serious."

Meghna's eyes lit up. "Do you think there's something up there?"

"Only one way to find out," Kurchi replied, already heading for the curtain in the corner of the rooftop room. Behind it was a narrow wooden door that creaked softly when opened. A musty scent wafted out—a mix of old paper and time itself.

The attic stairs were steep and narrow, lit faintly by the dying light through a small window at the top. As they climbed, their footsteps made soft thumps on the wood. When Kurchi pushed the door open, the space revealed itself like a long-lost memory.

Stacks of cardboard boxes lined the walls, old trunks sat with rusted hinges, and shelves groaned under the weight of forgotten books and wrapped-up artifacts. Cobwebs danced lazily in the corners. But there was no fear—only the thrill of discovery.

“It smells like Uncle’s stories,” Ghurni said, brushing her fingers along the edge of a dusty globe.

Kurchi moved with purpose toward the back of the attic, drawn to a large wooden chest carved with faded designs. She ran her hand over its surface, brushing away a layer of dust. A symbol slowly emerged beneath her touch—a treble clef, an eye, and a flame.

“Have you ever seen this before?” she asked.

Ghurni and Meghna stepped closer. Meghna’s brow furrowed. “That was in the story. On the cover of the book hidden in the library.”

Kurchi's heart beat faster. Carefully, she unlatched the chest and opened it. The hinges groaned, but inside it was dry and neat. Among yellowed scrolls and aged parchment sat a single book. Its cover was dark and leathery, with no title—only that same symbol engraved faintly on its front.

The moment Kurchi touched it, a current passed through the air, and the attic seemed to hold its breath. The book pulsed softly under her fingers, like it was alive.

“Did you feel that?” she whispered.

Ghurni nodded slowly. “It’s... humming.”

Meghna leaned in. “Open it.”

Kurchi did. The pages inside were covered in script she couldn’t read—letters that seemed to shift slightly when she looked directly at them. The air grew cooler, and the attic dimmer, as though the book had changed the room around them.

“It’s magic,” Meghna said quietly.

“Or something close to it,” Kurchi whispered.

Ghurni squinted at the page. “It’s reacting to you. Like it knows you.”

Kurchi stared at the mysterious text. She didn’t understand the words, but something in her did. She could feel the call of it deep in her chest.

“I think this is the beginning,” she said, closing the book gently. “Of something we’re supposed to discover.”

Ghurni folded her arms. “You think it’s all real? The story, the book, the lost library?”

“I don’t know,” Kurchi admitted. “But doesn’t it feel like it?”

Meghna nodded. “We found the symbol. We found the book. That can’t be a coincidence.”

They stood in silence, the weight of the moment settling around them like dust.

“Let’s come back tomorrow,” Kurchi said, tucking the book into her sling bag. “We’ll figure it out. Together.”

As they left the attic and stepped back into the familiar comfort of the rooftop room, the evening breeze stirred the chimes at the window. The melody rang faintly... almost like a whisper from the pages they’d just discovered.

Chapter 3
Singing to the Pages

The following day seemed to drag on for Kurchi, Ghurni, and Meghna. Each class, each passing minute felt like an eternity, as their minds were preoccupied with the mysterious book they had discovered the previous evening. They couldn't stop thinking about it. Kurchi could feel the book's weight in her backpack, as if it were calling to her, beckoning her to uncover its secrets.

When the final bell rang, signaling the end of the school day, the three girls rushed out of the school gates and began the familiar walk back to Kurchi's house. The air was still warm, a hint of the summer evening lingering, but the weight of anticipation was heavier than the heat.

As they entered the house, they were greeted by the usual hum of activity. Kurchi's father was in the kitchen, preparing a snack—his culinary skills always a treat for the girls. The scent of freshly baked parathas filled the air.

"Ah, there you are, my three favorite adventurers," Kurchi's father called, grinning as he placed the snacks on the kitchen table. "I made you all some snacks. I'm guessing you've had a long day at school?"

The girls exchanged a glance, trying to hide their excitement.

"Thanks, Papa," Kurchi said, taking a seat at the table. "These smell amazing."

Ghurni eagerly reached for a paratha. "So, what's for dinner tonight?" she asked, her voice casual but her eyes flickering with curiosity.

Kurchi's father leaned against the counter. "I haven't decided yet, but first, you all must eat. You can't go on an adventure without some fuel, right?"

The girls laughed, but their minds weren't really on the food. They had an unspoken agreement—today, after they ate, they were going straight to the attic.

The trio finished their snacks quickly, then excused themselves and made their way up the stairs to Kurchi's rooftop room. The atmosphere inside the room was different today. It felt charged, as though something important was about to happen.

Kurchi led the way, her steps light as she climbed the stairs. Ghurni and Meghna followed closely behind. The sun had just begun to dip behind the horizon, casting a soft glow on the room.

They sat down in the middle of the floor, surrounding the chest where the book had been. Kurchi, with a sense of reverence, pulled the book out of her backpack and placed it gently in front of her. The book seemed to hum, its soft vibrations resonating with the girls' curiosity.

"I keep thinking about it," Kurchi said, her voice soft. "It's so strange. It's like the book is… alive somehow."

Ghurni leaned forward, her brow furrowed. "You mean the way it reacted when you touched it? It felt like it was waiting for something, like it wanted us to open it."

Meghna, who had been sitting quietly, spoke up. "What if… What if it's trying to tell us something? We need to figure out how to read it."

Kurchi nodded, her fingers tracing the strange symbol on the cover—the treble clef, the eye, and the flame. It seemed to glow faintly as her touch lingered. "I don't know if we're ready for whatever's inside, but… I think we need to try."

Ghurni looked at Kurchi. "You've got this, Kurchi. Whatever it is, we can figure it out together."

Kurchi took a deep breath and opened the book. As the cover creaked open, the room seemed to hold its breath. The pages inside were covered with strange symbols and diagrams, none of which the girls could understand. But as Kurchi flipped through the pages, her gaze lingered on one particular page.

It wasn't like the others. This one was blank, but the moment her eyes fell upon it, the page began to glow softly. The words began to appear—words that weren't there before.

"Sing," the page said in delicate script.

Kurchi looked at Ghurni and Meghna, both of whom were staring at the book in stunned silence. "Did you see that?" Kurchi whispered.

Ghurni leaned in closer. "It says 'Sing.'"

"What should we sing?" Kurchi asked, her voice trembling.

Meghna, always the more thoughtful one, suggested softly, "What if it's a song you know? Maybe something from when you were little. Like… a lullaby?"

Kurchi closed her eyes, recalling the lullaby her mother had sung to her when she was a child. It was a simple melody, one that always made her feel safe. She didn't hesitate. She began to sing, her voice rising and falling with the soft rhythm of the lullaby.

As the first few notes filled the room, something extraordinary happened. The book shuddered in her hands. The pages began to turn on their own, fluttering like leaves in the wind. The sound of her voice seemed to vibrate through the very air around them, causing the walls of the room to hum in response. It was as if the entire room had come alive with her song.

As she continued to sing, a faint glow appeared on the page of the book. The words she had seen earlier began to rearrange themselves, transforming into a riddle.

"Through voice and heart, the path you'll find,

The keys to the past are yours to bind.

Solve the song, unlock the door,

What is lost, you'll restore."

Kurchi's voice faltered slightly as she read the riddle aloud. Ghurni's eyes lit up with excitement. "That's it! That's the clue!"

Meghna, who had been silent until now, looked at the book with awe. "It's asking us to solve a song. A riddle through your voice."

"But what does it mean?" Kurchi asked, the words of the riddle echoing in her mind. "What is lost? What door do we unlock?"

The room grew quieter as they all tried to make sense of the riddle. The answer was elusive, slipping just beyond their reach, like a dream fading at dawn.

Ghurni was leaning over the book, her eyes scanning the glowing riddle again. "Through voice and heart, the path you'll find... What's lost, you'll restore…" She tapped her chin, thinking. "I'm guessing this means we need to go somewhere. Find something that's been lost."

Meghna, who had been sitting silently, spoke up. "And the door? What's that supposed to mean?"

Kurchi shook her head. "I'm not sure. But I think the next step is right here." She opened the book, and as she did, the pages turned on their own again. A soft hum filled the room, and the same glow appeared. But this time, it was different.

Instead of another riddle, the page revealed something that took their breath away: a map.

It was a map of their own town, but not quite. There were familiar streets, buildings, and parks, but certain places were marked with glowing, faintly pulsing dots. Some of the landmarks they recognized—like the school, the river, and the town square—were all there, but there were also areas they'd never seen before. Dark, mysterious spots that seemed to pulse with an otherworldly light.

Kurchi couldn't tear her eyes away from the map. "Is this… our town?" she asked, her voice a whisper.

Ghurni leaned in closely, her gaze moving over the map. "It's definitely our town. Look, there's the school, and there's the river we always walk by." She pointed to a spot near the riverbank. "But this… this place here? I've never seen this building before."

Meghna was already looking for something else. "And these marks—are they the dots?" she asked, pointing to the small glowing markers scattered around the map. "Each of these has a glow around it. It's like they're calling to us."

"Maybe they're the places we need to go," Kurchi said, her voice filled with awe. "Maybe these are the doors the riddle was talking about."

Kurchi looked from the glowing map to her friends, her resolve hardening. "Let's figure this out, together. Tomorrow, we'll follow this map. We'll find the door the book is guiding us to."

Ghurni and Meghna nodded. The three of them had always faced the world together, and now, with the book and map in hand, they knew their real adventure was only just beginning.

Chapter 4
The Hidden Library

The next day passed in a blur. The girls couldn't focus on their classes—every moment was consumed by thoughts of the map and the adventure they were about to embark on. When the school bell rang, they rushed out, eager to start their quest.

They met at Kurchi's house and, with a shared sense of determination, headed towards the river. The walk there was quiet, each of them feeling the weight of the unknown pressing down on them.

As they approached the abandoned building, the air seemed to grow cooler. The structure loomed ahead, dilapidated and weathered by time. It was a large, two-story building, with cracked windows and vines creeping up the sides. The place looked like it hadn't been touched in years. But there was something strange about it, something that made Kurchi's stomach flutter with anticipation.

"This is it," she said, her voice barely above a whisper.

Ghurni, ever the brave one, led the way to the front door. "Let's go in. The map says this is where we start."

Meghna hesitated. "Are we sure we should go inside? It looks pretty dangerous."

Kurchi turned to her. "We have to. This is where the adventure begins. And whatever's hidden inside might be the answer we're looking for."

With a deep breath, Meghna nodded, and the three of them pushed open the creaking door.

The old door groaned as it swung open, revealing a narrow hallway wrapped in shadows and silence. A breath of cool, dusty air greeted the three girls, stirring something ancient in the air. At the threshold stood Kurchi, her heart thudding in her chest as she stared into the mysterious corridor. Behind her, Meghna and Ghurni exchanged uneasy glances, their curiosity battling with a quiet fear.

The only light came from flickering candles embedded in cracked stone walls. Strange symbols—ones they had seen on the map and inside the ancient books—were carved along the hallway. They seemed to glow softly, as if alive, pulsing with energy that called to them.

Kurchi took a cautious step forward, the soles of her shoes whispering against the dust-covered floor. A strange pull tugged at her chest, like the building itself was inviting her in. Meghna followed close behind, her eyes darting from shadow to shadow. Ghurni's voice, barely louder than a whisper, broke the silence.

"Do you feel that?" she asked, her voice tight with awe.

"Yeah," Meghna replied, scanning the walls. "It's like… someone's watching."

Kurchi didn't answer. She felt it too—an invisible presence, unsettling but not entirely hostile. Still, something deep inside urged her to press on.

They moved together down the corridor, their footsteps echoing in the dimness. At the far end, two tall wooden doors awaited them. They were carved with the same ancient symbols, but these were different—each design glowed faintly, in rhythm with their heartbeats.

Kurchi reached out, her fingers brushing the wood. The doors creaked open slowly, revealing a room that stole the breath from their lungs.

A vast underground library stretched before them.

Rows upon rows of ancient books and scrolls lined the towering shelves, their worn bindings whispering secrets of a time long forgotten. The ceiling arched high above, glowing orbs hovering near its peak, bathing the space in a soft, bluish light. It was silent, save for the quiet hum of magic in the air.

Kurchi gasped. “This… this is incredible.”

Ghurni turned in a slow circle, eyes wide. “It’s like we’ve stepped into a secret the world forgot.”

Even cautious Meghna couldn’t hide her wonder—but her voice trembled. “Are we… supposed to be here?”

“We have to be,” Kurchi said firmly. “This is part of the path. I can feel it.”

They ventured deeper into the library, walking slowly across the creaking wooden floor. Dust danced in the air, stirred by their movement. Kurchi ran her fingers over a row of ancient books. Some had no titles. Others were etched with symbols they now recognized—the same ones from the map and the hallway.

Suddenly, Meghna cried out, “Look at that!”

She pointed to a glowing pedestal in the center of the room. The girls rushed over.

The pedestal was carved from smooth stone, its surface covered in familiar symbols: a flame, a treble clef, and an eye. At its center sat a single book, its dark leather cover shimmering faintly as though it were untouched by time.

Kurchi reached for it. The moment her fingers made contact, the book snapped open. Its pages fluttered wildly, then stopped, settling on one that vibrated with hidden power.

A hum filled the room, and the girls leaned closer. Words written in an ancient script glowed softly.

Ghurni peered at the page. "I think I can read this. It's from the myths I've studied."

Kurchi pulled out her notebook, scribbling quickly. "What does it say?"

Ghurni read aloud:

"Three symbols guard the path ahead,

The flame, the clef, the eye are led,

Each will guide, each will see,

Only when united, will you be free."

Kurchi looked down at the pedestal. "The treble clef, the flame, and the eye. We've seen them. On the map, the walls… They must mean something."

Meghna examined the carvings more closely. "There are indentations here. Like something's supposed to go in."

Ghurni nodded slowly. "Or… maybe something we have to do. The poem said we have to be united."

Kurchi's eyes lit up. "It matches us. My voice. Your riddles. Meghna's… gift. Let's try."

Kurchi stepped forward first. Her gaze fixed on the treble clef. She closed her eyes, drew a deep breath, and began to hum—a soft, melodic tune that filled the room like sunlight breaking through fog. The clef symbol began to glow, resonating with her voice. Warmth spread from the stone, and the indentation around the clef filled with brilliant light.

Ghurni stared in awe. "Your voice… it unlocked it."

Kurchi smiled. "One down."

Next was Ghurni. She stepped up to the eye symbol. As her fingers touched the stone, glowing words appeared on the pedestal:

"I am always in front of you, but you cannot see me. What am I?"

Ghurni thought for a moment. Her brow furrowed. Then her eyes lit up. "The future."

The eye symbol blazed with light, and the pedestal rumbled softly beneath her.

"I did it!" she whispered.

Meghna approached the flame, uncertain. "I don't know what to do…"

"You can," Kurchi said gently.

Meghna closed her eyes and focused. Slowly, warmth flowed through her fingertips. A faint glow flickered in her palm, like a tiny ember taking life. The flame symbol responded instantly, flaring up as if awakened. The final indentation filled with light.

The pedestal trembled.

With a soft groan, a hidden door in the back of the library swung open, revealing a narrow passage.

The girls turned to each other, breathless.

"This is it," Kurchi whispered. "We're about to discover something incredible."

And, side by side, the three friends stepped into the unknown.

Chapter 5
A Trail of Riddles

The passage was long and winding, carved from ancient stone. The walls were lined with strange symbols that seemed to move if you looked away for too long. It felt like the hallway itself was alive, watching them. The air grew colder with every step, and the dim lights flickered like tiny fireflies trapped in the stone.

"Do you see that?" Meghna whispered, pointing at the walls.

Ghurni nodded, eyes squinting at the shifting shapes. "It's like the symbols are… changing."

Kurchi reached out a hand but didn't touch them. "I think it's magic. Old magic."

The hallway stretched on and on, until they finally stopped in front of a tall stone door covered in intricate carvings. Each image told a different story—warriors, temples, strange creatures. But in the center of the door was a glowing riddle written in an ancient script.

Ghurni leaned closer. "I can read this... sort of."

She traced the lines with her finger, reading aloud:

"The past cannot be seen,

The future is just a dream.

The present is what matters,

And where you stand, you will be the key."

The girls stared at the words.

"It's about time," Meghna said slowly. "But what does it want us to do?"

They sat in silence, thinking. Ghurni looked at the carvings again, as if hoping they would speak to her. Meghna closed her eyes, trying to feel the answer. Kurchi placed a hand on the door and whispered, "We are here, now. This is the moment."

The door trembled.

A warm glow spread through the carvings. Then, with a soft click, the stone door began to slide open.

"The key... was the present," Kurchi said, blinking in surprise. "It wanted us to understand that being here, now, matters."

The door revealed a new chamber, much larger than the last. But it wasn't just a room—it was a maze. Tall walls twisted in every direction, and in every corner was another puzzle. A heavy stone block that had to be moved just right. A set of glowing tiles that needed to be stepped on in a perfect pattern. Riddles written on hanging banners. Some puzzles tested their minds, others their instincts.

They worked together, using everything they had learned. Ghurni studied the riddles and decoded the ancient language. Meghna's sharp senses helped them notice details others might miss—small cracks, hidden buttons, or whispers in the stone. Kurchi's voice kept them steady, singing softly when they grew tired or nervous. Somehow, her songs made the room feel less scary, more alive.

They moved deeper into the maze until they found a mirror. It was tall and dusty, with a cloudy surface that shimmered like fog. As they stepped closer, words began to appear on the glass.

“To find what you seek,

Look into the past,

Remember the moments,

When your heart was steadfast.”

Another riddle.

“It wants us to remember something,” Ghurni said. “Something important. Something true.”

The girls sat in front of the mirror and closed their eyes.

Kurchi remembered the old park near her house, where they first played together as little kids. Ghurni thought of the time they got lost on the way home and held hands the whole time, never letting go. Meghna remembered building their rooftop club—the day they promised to be best friends forever.

“It was that day in the park,” Kurchi said quietly, eyes misty. “When we found that old tree and carved our names into the bark. We knew we’d always stick together.”

The mirror glowed bright. The cloudy surface cleared, revealing a hidden tunnel behind it. And in the reflection, a new riddle appeared—just a glimpse—before fading away.

But something else changed, too.

The room felt different. The air tingled. The floor beneath their feet seemed to hum. And then, faintly, they heard it—whispers.

The library was watching.

They moved carefully now, nerves on edge. Shadows shifted across the walls. The lights dimmed. Something—or someone—was nearby.

They turned a corner and came face-to-face with a shadowy figure.

It wasn't quite human, but not a monster either. It looked like a guardian made of shadows and smoke, with glowing eyes that seemed to see right through them.

The guardian spoke in a voice that echoed everywhere at once. "Do you understand the riddles? Have you learned what truly matters?"

It paused, then whispered another riddle:

"The mind alone cannot see,

The heart alone cannot lead,

But together they will guide you,

To what you truly need."

The girls stood silently, hearts pounding.

Ghurni spoke first. "We've used our minds to solve the puzzles."

Meghna nodded. "And our hearts to trust each other."

Kurchi stepped forward, her voice calm. "We needed both. That's how we got this far."

The guardian didn't answer—but it smiled.

And then, with a swirl of shadows, it vanished.

In its place, a glowing doorway appeared. Inside was a round chamber. In the middle of it stood a pedestal. On the pedestal, a small compass spun slowly, its needle glowing gold.

They had found it.

Kurchi reached out and picked it up. The compass was warm in her hand, and the needle pointed toward something far beyond the chamber. A stone basin surrounded by a ring of faded carvings.

Chapter 6
A Whisper from the Past

“I feel like… it’s waiting for us to look,” Meghna said, nodding toward the basin.

The girls approached the stone circle together. The basin, carved from obsidian and etched with golden script, was now filled with something between smoke and liquid light. It shimmered like a reflection from a dream. And then, slowly, the mist inside began to swirl.

The mist spun faster until it formed a whirlpool of light. Then, like a screen of water parting, it cleared to reveal an image: a young boy, about their age, stood in a clearing surrounded by wild bamboo groves. He wore clothes from a different time—an old cotton kurta and trousers—and carried a satchel made of thick cloth slung over his shoulder. Behind him stood a group of children, each different in age and appearance. One held a staff, another a glowing compass, and one—a girl with thick braids—had a voice that echoed like thunder when she spoke.

“This… is in Bengal,” Kurchi whispered, recognizing the flora, the shape of the trees, even the reddish tint of the soil. “Look at the ground. It’s near the old riverbanks.”

“They were like us,” Ghurni murmured, eyes locked on the vision.

The boy turned, looking straight toward them—though it wasn’t possible, was it? And then the vision spoke, though his lips barely moved.

“To those who find this place: we are the Keepers. Once, long ago, we were chosen by the Library. We were children, too, when we first found the book that could only be sung open. We were the ones before you.”

The girls leaned in closer.

“The world has forgotten the magic of knowledge, of stories, of truth. The Library sleeps when it is no longer needed… and awakens only when danger comes again. If you have found it, then you are the next.”

As the boy’s voice faded, the mist in the basin rippled again.
Behind the boy’s figure, faint letters began to appear along the curved stone edge of the basin. The words shimmered softly, almost hidden in the swirling light. Kurchi leaned in, and without thinking, began to read aloud:

"When the Voices grow silent, and the Flames forget their warmth, and the Eyes close to the truth, three shall arise—bound not by blood, but by bond. One who sings the stones awake. One who sees the riddles within shadows. One who guards the ember of memory. Together, they shall mend the broken song of the world, or watch it fall into endless night."

The letters faded as quickly as they had appeared, leaving only a faint warmth in the stone.

The girls exchanged glances, uneasy but silent. They didn’t understand what the words meant.

The boy’s image wavered, and a new vision took shape—this time of a powerful storm. Pages flew like birds across the sky. A monstrous figure, cloaked in shadow, walked through the forest, books crumbling beneath its feet. It touched a tree, and the tree turned to ash.

But the boy's voice continued, sharper now:

"The Unwritten are ancient — a force born from forgetting — but they cannot break the Library's heart unless a Guardian first falls. Only through a broken Keeper can the flood of forgetting spill across the world. Beware the one who forgets his song, for he shall open the way."

In the swirling mist, faint shapes gathered — not fully formed, not yet unleashed — as if waiting for a door to open.

“A great forgetting is coming,” the vision continued. “There are those who wish to erase memory, to destroy wisdom, to silence every voice. They are the Unwritten. And they are rising.”

Kurchi’s hands trembled. Her voice came out in a whisper. “Unwritten?”

“They’re… the opposite of what we are,” Ghurni said, her tone suddenly serious. “If we’re chosen to protect knowledge, they’re the ones who destroy it.”

The basin shimmered again, showing a glowing symbol that matched the pedestal in the other room—a treble clef, an eye, and a flame. But now, the flame was flickering dangerously, almost extinguished.

The boy in the vision reappeared. His eyes were grave.

“The Library has waited long enough. If you hear this message, you must remember: A Guardian has fallen. Restore the Guardian before he opens the door.”

The image dissolved. Silence returned.

The girls stood there for a long time.

“I thought we were just exploring,” Meghna finally said, her voice small.

“We were,” Kurchi replied, her gaze locked on the now-empty basin. “But now it’s something else.”

Ghurni stepped back from the basin and began pacing slowly, processing. “So there were other children before us. Guardians. And now we’ve been chosen because the danger is coming back.”

Kurchi looked at the basin again. “What does it mean to protect knowledge?”

Meghna sat down on the floor beside the pedestal. “Maybe it means we have to stop the Guardian.”

There was a long pause.

“And that’s why the book came to us,” Kurchi whispered. “That’s why it hummed when I sang to it.”

Ghurni opened her satchel and pulled out the glowing book. As soon as she touched it, the pages flipped on their own, settling on the map they’d seen before—only now, it was much more detailed.

Meghna gasped. “It’s changed!”

The familiar town map now included hidden pathways, old buildings, secret gardens, and a strange emblem at the far corner of the page—a circle containing few shapes.

“There’s more to this than just the library,” Ghurni said, her eyes scanning the map. “This is just one piece.”

Kurchi traced a line from their current location on the map to a point marked with a quill and ink symbol. "Maybe this is where we go next."

Meghna peered closer. "It looks like the old mansion ruins near the east fields. No one ever goes there."

"Then that's where we go," Kurchi said, a spark of determination in her voice.

As they followed the glowing path back through the underground passages, the library slowly dimmed behind them, its doors gently closing.

They emerged into the evening light on Kurchi's rooftop. It was nearly dusk. The sun was a melted orange on the horizon, casting golden streaks across the clouds.

Kurchi's father was there, a plate of pakoras in hand and a kettle of hot tea by his side.

"There you are," he said, as if they had only stepped into the attic for a moment. "You girls missed snack time."

He handed out the food as they gathered around their usual rooftop spot. The magic book, now looking like an ordinary journal again, lay quietly on the table beside them.

Kurchi's father poured tea into three tiny cups. "I used to come up here as a boy and read old stories. Some of them felt more real than anything else. Almost like the books were watching me."

Kurchi looked up sharply. "Did you ever find a book… that sang when someone sang to it?"

Her father smiled, a twinkle in his eye. “Not exactly. But I’ve found books that spoke louder than words.”

Ghurni raised an eyebrow at Kurchi, who said nothing more. Meghna chewed a pakora, deep in thought.

“Did you ever hear of children who protected stories?” Ghurni asked.

He paused for just a moment—barely a blink—before answering, “Some stories are so old, even the stars forget them.”

After her father left them alone again, the girls sat quietly, the setting sun painting their faces in honeyed gold.

“We’re in this together, right?” Kurchi said. “Whatever comes next, we figure it out together.”

Ghurni nodded. “Of course.”

Meghna added, “And we never stop asking questions.”

They stretched out their pinky fingers and linked them—just as they’d done since kindergarten.

“Pinky oath,” they whispered together. “We protect what must not be forgotten.”

The wind lifted the edge of the magical book’s cover.

A new page had appeared.

Chapter 7
The Compass of Voices

The rooftop was unusually quiet the next morning. A soft drizzle kissed the tiles, and the smell of wet earth filled the air as the three girls huddled inside Kurchi's rooftop room, the magical book spread open on a patchwork quilt.

The new title shimmered faintly: "Chapter Two: The Compass of Voices."

They hadn't dared to turn the page last night, but the book hadn't waited. Overnight, it had written itself again. The next steps. The next mystery.

Ghurni tapped the title. "Do you think it means a real compass?"

"Or something symbolic," Meghna said. "Voices. Maybe singing? Maybe Kurchi again?"

Kurchi looked thoughtful. "It could mean anything. But there's one way to find out." She turned the page.

The parchment felt thicker than before, edged in gold, and the ink shimmered green. At the center of the page was a circle divided into four parts. Each section bore a musical symbol, a riddle, and a name in a script they didn't recognize. Beneath the circle, a glowing sentence stood out:

"The Compass finds those who listen. The Voice begins the journey. The Eye solves the way. The Flame remembers."

Kurchi, Ghurni, and Meghna exchanged glances.

"That's us," Ghurni said. "The Voice… Kurchi. The Eye… me. The Flame… you, Meghna."

Meghna frowned. "Why am I the flame, though?"

"You remember things. You see what others forget," Ghurni explained. "Memory is like fire. It warms, it lights the way. And sometimes, it burns away lies."

Kurchi traced the compass on the page. "Look. Each section points to a direction. North, south, east, west. Maybe it's showing us a path?"

"And here," Ghurni added, pointing to the center, "there's a musical note… but it also looks like a key."

Just then, the rooftop door creaked. Kurchi's father peeked his head in, balancing a tray of freshly baked coconut narus and three tumblers of chilled aam panna.

"Morning, mystery girls," he said, stepping into the room. "What's the puzzle today?"

They scrambled to hide the book—but not fast enough. He smiled knowingly. "Still that old book, huh? Must be something special."

Kurchi hesitated. She didn't want to lie. "It is. It's sort of… guiding us through something."

Her father raised an eyebrow but said nothing. He set the tray down and sat beside them. "I used to love stories about magical compasses," he said, taking a sweet. "There's a tale from old Bengal about a whispering one. You sang to it, and it would hum in response. The right tune would unlock the right path."

The girls froze.

"Where did you hear that story?" Kurchi asked quickly.

He laughed. “Oh, from your dadu, of course. He had books you wouldn’t believe. Ancient stuff. Some of it probably nonsense. But good nonsense.”

He studied their faces for a moment. “Are you sure you’re not in the middle of one of those stories?”

There was a pause.

“We might be,” Kurchi said quietly.

Her father smiled but didn’t press. “Then eat first. Adventures need fuel.” He left them alone with the sweets, but his words lingered.

Kurchi hummed softly as she stared again at the compass on the page. just a few notes from a rural folk song her mother loved. As she hummed, the parchment glowed. The musical symbol at the north point shimmered—and then the ink rearranged itself into a new shape: a map. A path unfurled from their rooftop, over the neighborhood, into a dense green patch labeled The Grove of Lost Songs.

“What just happened?” Meghna gasped.

“You sang it open,” Ghurni said. “Just like when the book opened the first time.”

Kurchi tried humming a different tune—nothing happened. But the lullaby worked again, revealing a small cottage deep in the grove.

“This is it,” she whispered. “Our next destination.”

They packed quickly: water bottles, snacks, notebooks, a compass, a torch, and the magical book tucked in Kurchi’s sling pouch. Sneakers on, hair tied back. The drizzle had stopped, but the mist still lingered.

Kurchi told her father they were heading to the old orchard. Not quite a lie.

He handed them an extra packet of homemade puffed rice mixture. “Share and stay close,” he said, brushing a smudge from Kurchi’s cheek. “And if you find a singing compass, you know who to call.”

“Promise,” Kurchi grinned.

They waved goodbye and slipped down the stairs, hearts fluttering in rhythm with the quiet, electric call of the unknown.

It took forty minutes on foot, past the small canal bridge and overgrown paddy fields, to reach the grove. It was an ancient patch of woodland, spoken of in stories, whispered about in lullabies. As they stepped inside, the world changed. Birdsong faded. In its place, soft musical notes floated—everywhere and nowhere at once.

“I don’t like this,” Meghna whispered, clutching Ghurni’s sleeve.

Ghurni glanced at the compass they’d brought—it spun wildly in her palm. “It’s reacting to something.”

Kurchi took a breath and began to hum the lullaby again. The trees rustled in response. A breeze circled around them. And then—a glowing ribbon of light appeared, floating through the grove like a will-o’-the-wisp.

“It’s showing us the way,” Kurchi said.

They followed the glowing thread in silence, weaving through bamboo and ancient banyan roots until they came upon a small, weather-worn cottage.

It looked long abandoned, but there was no dust inside. It smelled of sandalwood and ink. Scrolls lined the walls. On a wooden table rested a music box with a carved bird perched on top. Kurchi touched it.

It sprang to life, playing the same lullaby—but beneath the melody, a voice whispered: "You have come with the Voice. The Compass is near."

A drawer under the table slid open.

Inside was a silver pendant shaped like a compass. The same four-part symbol from the book was engraved on it. As Kurchi reached out, it floated gently into her hand. The music box stopped. The compass spun once and pointed west.

Another path had opened.

As they stepped outside, the grove came alive with whispering voices. The trees sang—not just notes, but words, ancient and familiar. And then, clearly: "Follow the echo. Find the first Temple. The Voice must awaken the flame."

Kurchi's heart skipped. "The first temple?"

Ghurni opened the book again. A new page had appeared. "The Forgotten Temple lies beyond the river and beneath the roots. Let the compass lead. Let memory burn. Let riddles solve the gate."

"We're heading toward something big," Meghna said, her voice quiet.

"Then we go together," Kurchi said.

“And we protect what must not be forgotten,” Ghurni added.

The compass pendant glowed faintly against Kurchi’s chest. Without another word, they turned west and began to walk.

Chapter 8
Across the River, Beneath the Roots

The sun peeked out shyly from behind a sheet of clouds as Kurchi, Ghurni, and Meghna followed the magical compass through the narrow path. The silver pendant in Kurchi's hand glowed softly, like it was excited for what came next. Tall sugarcane plants lined both sides of the trail, their long green leaves whispering in the wind, almost like they were speaking a secret language.

The girls didn't know exactly where they were going, but the compass seemed sure. So they kept walking, trusting its silent pull. After nearly an hour, the muddy path led them to a wide clearing. The ground sloped down into a shallow valley, and there—shimmering under the trees—was a quiet brown river.

Kurchi squinted. "This isn't on any of our school maps."

Meghna nodded. "I remember my dad once said there used to be a river in this town. Maybe this is what's left."

Ghurni stepped closer to the edge. "The compass still points forward. We need to cross."

They walked along the riverbank, looking for a way across. No bridge. No boat. But then Ghurni spotted something strange in the distance. "Look at that tree!"

It was a giant banyan tree, its roots twisted and stretched across the river like a tangled web. Some of the roots were so thick and strong, they looked like they could hold their weight.

"The book said, 'beneath the roots,'" Kurchi said. "This has to be the place."

They checked the roots carefully. Solid and steady. Kurchi went first, arms out for balance. The compass glowed brighter with each step. Ghurni followed, mumbling a riddle under her breath—her favorite way to stay calm. Meghna came last, her eyes scanning the quiet river and the trees around them.

Once they were across, the compass needle did something strange—it pointed straight down.

"We're standing right above something," said Kurchi.

The three girls searched around the giant tree, brushing away moss and leaves. Ghurni found a hollow space beneath the roots. Meghna tapped it—it echoed!

Kurchi brushed more dirt away and found a stone door hidden under the roots. It was carved with strange symbols—tiny music notes, flames, and puzzle shapes.

"Our symbols again," whispered Ghurni.

Kurchi took a deep breath and sang the soft lullaby. Nothing happened.

"Wait," said Ghurni. "There's something written here." She read the riddle carved into the stone:

"Three flames guide the silent song.

A voice, a memory, a mind made strong.

Speak your names, and let truth rise—

Only then will the temple open its eyes."

The girls looked at each other. Was it really asking for them?

Kurchi stepped forward. “I am Kurchi. The Voice.”

“I am Ghurni. The Eye,” said Ghurni.

Meghna straightened up. “I am Meghna. The Flame.”

The stone trembled beneath their feet. The vines curled away. With a low rumble, the trapdoor slowly sank into the earth, revealing a spiral staircase leading into darkness.

A cold breeze rushed up from below.

“Well,” said Ghurni, pulling out her little flashlight, “here we go again.”

Down they went, one by one. The compass pendant glowed softly, lighting the way when the flashlight flickered. The air smelled old, like dusty books that hadn’t been opened in a hundred years.

At the bottom, they found a huge round room. It was lit by glowing crystals on the walls, their light bouncing like stars in a cave. Pillars shaped like trees stretched toward a high ceiling they couldn’t even see.

In the middle of the room stood a stone table. Something was resting on it, wrapped in old silk.

Kurchi stepped closer. The compass in her hand buzzed gently.

Ghurni picked up the silk bundle and unwrapped it carefully. Inside was a wooden box with a golden latch.

Suddenly, the compass floated from Kurchi’s palm and clicked onto the box’s latch. It snapped open by itself.

Inside was a strange book—its cover dark green, its spine stitched with glowing silver thread. The title sparkled in light:

"The Voicekeeper's Guide."

As soon as Kurchi touched the book, music filled her mind. Not just a song, but hundreds of notes, chants, and words she didn't know but somehow understood. It was like opening a door inside her heart.

Then, a deep voice echoed through the chamber.

"Welcome, Voice. Welcome, Eye. Welcome, Flame.

Long have you been awaited.

You are not the first. You are not the last.

But you are needed now more than ever."

The girls froze. Who was speaking?

"We are the memory of the Keepers," the voice continued, soft and wise. "We guide. We guard.

The Compass has awakened.

The Heartstone sleeps still.

The Temple trials will test your unity.

Only then may you reach the next library."

Kurchi opened the book. The pages turned by themselves until they stopped at a map. three glowing Xs marked places across the page, all connected by winding lines.

"There are three temples," said Ghurni, counting.

But before they could say more, the crystals dimmed. A strange dark shape formed on the far wall. It looked like a puddle of ink, swirling and growing like it was alive.

A voice hissed from the shadow.

“Too soon… they are too young…

The Seal must not break…

The Flame must not remember…”

Then the shadow vanished. The room fell silent again.

The girls stared at each other, hearts pounding.

“What… was that?” Ghurni asked in a whisper.

“A warning,” Meghna said, her voice shaking.

“Or a threat,” Kurchi added.

Whatever it was, someone—or something—had seen them. And it wasn’t happy.

By the time they climbed back out into the sunlight, the river was still and peaceful again, like nothing had changed. The banyan tree stood quietly, hiding its secrets once more.

They crossed the root bridge in silence, feeling the weight of everything they had seen.

Back at Kurchi’s house, the smell of hot singara and sweet chutney greeted them on the rooftop. Her father smiled, setting down plates.

“Your timing is perfect,” he said.

He didn’t ask where they had been. But as they ate, he told a story.

“Long ago,” he said, “this town had whispering stones. Some say they were left behind by children. Others say they came from the earth itself. But they were always found by the curious.”

Kurchi looked at her friends. Her backpack, resting beside her chair, held the Voicekeeper’s Guide. The compass was quiet for now. But on the map inside the book, the next path was already glowing.

Chapter 9
The First Trial Begins

The next morning was warm and quiet, with a little bit of mist floating over the rooftops like sleepy clouds. Kurchi lay in bed, staring at the ceiling. She couldn't stop thinking about the strange things that had happened yesterday—the whispering chamber, the magical book called the Voicekeeper's Guide, and that scary warning from the shadowy figure.

At breakfast, her father gave her a warm bowl of fluffy luchis with potato curry and said with a smile, "Still thinking about that old banyan tree?"

Kurchi blinked in surprise. "How do you know we were there?"

Her father smiled mysteriously. "Roots hold many secrets," he said. "They can take you places no map can find." Then he got up and walked into his study, humming a soft tune. Kurchi didn't know the song—but somehow, it felt important.

That afternoon, golden sunlight filled their little rooftop room. Ghurni was the first to arrive, holding a bunch of notes in her hands.

"I read the whole section on maps in the Voicekeeper's Guide," she said excitedly. "Every magical temple has a trial. This one is called the Trial of Unity."

Just then, Meghna climbed the stairs, carrying a box of homemade snacks—sweet shingaras and mango sandesh. "Trial of Unity?" she said, grinning. "Sounds like a group project. Only... scarier!"

Kurchi took out the compass pendant from around her neck. The moment she touched it, the needle spun in circles—then stopped, pointing toward the northeast. A glowing dot had appeared on the map in their book, marking a small hill at the edge of town, near the forest and some old mango trees.

“Let’s go,” Kurchi said. “We have to get there before sunset.”

They hopped on their bicycles and rode past their school, past the old temple with broken statues, and onto a dusty road lined with tall trees. The air smelled sweet—like ripe mangoes and the earth after rain. The hill wasn’t very tall, but it was hidden behind thick bushes. At its base sat a large, flat rock. On it were the same symbols they had seen at the temple—an eye, a flame, and a voice.

“This must be the place,” Ghurni whispered.

Kurchi gently sang a short tune. At once, the rock shimmered and split open, revealing a secret staircase spiraling down into the hill.

“No time like the present,” Meghna said, stepping forward.

Together, the three girls went down into the unknown.

At the bottom of the stairs, they entered a huge, glowing chamber filled with floating mirrors. Some were tiny, like the ones in purses. Others were taller than doors. The air was cool and quiet, until a soft voice spoke.

“To pass the trial, you must see what you hide. Step forward and find what’s true inside.”

The mirrors started moving around them. At first, they showed only their faces. But soon, each mirror began to reveal something different—something personal.

Kurchi stepped up to the biggest mirror. She saw herself on stage, singing. But then—her voice cracked. The people in the crowd laughed. She gasped and stepped back.

Meghna's mirror showed her sitting alone in class, trying to remember answers while everyone else played outside. "That was before I got good at remembering things," she whispered.

Ghurni's mirror showed her during a school competition. She couldn't solve a puzzle, and her classmates looked disappointed. Even the teacher frowned. "I don't like thinking about that day," she said softly.

The voice spoke again. "Face your fear. Accept it. Only then may the mirror pass."

Kurchi took a deep breath and looked again. Her reflection looked scared—but then she sang quietly, with courage. The audience stopped laughing. The mirror shimmered... and disappeared.

Meghna closed her eyes, smiled at her past self, and the mirror vanished too.

Ghurni reached out to her trembling reflection and whispered, "It's okay." Her mirror melted like mist.

Suddenly, the chamber changed. Bright walls of light rose up, turning the room into a maze! Paths opened and closed like doors made of magic. Kurchi's compass pendant glowed again.

"This must be the next part," she said.

Then—a soft chime echoed. And just like that, the girls were in different parts of the maze!

"Kurchi?!" Meghna called.

"I'm here!" Ghurni answered.

But they couldn't see each other.

Then, music floated through the maze. It was a lullaby—the one Kurchi always sang. She started to hum it louder.

Meghna heard it and followed the sound. Ghurni remembered something from the book: "In echoes lie your friend's footsteps. In silence, you forget." She clapped once.

She heard two claps in return.

Meghna used her sharp memory to trace her way forward. She counted her steps and turned carefully—left, right, left.

Kurchi kept singing, her voice guiding them like a thread of light.

And finally—all three girls ran into each other in the center of the maze! They were out of breath but smiling, hands clasped tightly.

In the center of the glowing room stood a figure—not dark and shadowy, but bright and beautiful, like a mix of a child and a shining star.

"You did not walk alone," the figure said gently. "You did not forget one another. Your fears did not blind you. You are ready for the second trial."

It raised one hand, and from the light, a magical key appeared—silver and green, shaped like a blooming lotus.

"This is the Key of Memory," it said. "You'll need it to open the next gate."

One by one, the girls touched the key.

In a blink, the glowing chamber vanished. The hill, the maze, the mirrors—all gone like a dream.

They found themselves standing beside their bicycles at the edge of the mango orchard. The sky was orange now, with the sun almost setting. They rode home slowly, quiet but thoughtful.

Back at the rooftop, Kurchi's father had lemon soda and crunchy nimki waiting for them.

"Busy day?" he asked with a twinkle in his eye.

The girls nodded, still catching their breath.

He didn't say anything more. He just handed them notebooks and pens. "Write it all down," he said. "One day, you'll want to remember."

Kurchi glanced at the Voicekeeper's Guide.

Chapter 10
The Second Key

The wind was howling louder than usual that night.

Up in Kurchi's rooftop room, the three friends sat close together in a half-circle. In front of them lay the Voicekeeper's Guide, glowing softly with a golden light.

Kurchi's father stepped in, holding a flask of warm milk. He placed it beside the leftover puffed rice.

"Strange winds tonight," he said, glancing at the open window. "You girls should be careful. Winds carry whispers... and sometimes, whispers whisper back."

He ruffled Kurchi's hair gently and gave a small smile. But it didn't quite reach his eyes.

As he left the room, Meghna hurried to close the window. "Did he actually mean that?" she asked.

"Knowing your dad?" Ghurni said, raising an eyebrow. "Definitely."

Kurchi looked down at the Voicekeeper's Guide. A brand-new riddle had appeared on the page. It shimmered in green ink that sparkled like sunlight through leaves.

"Second the key where silence grows,

Beneath the place where nothing flows.

Seek the roots beneath the stone,

Where one may speak who stands alone."

Ghurni leaned in, thinking hard. "That sounds like... the dried-up well. The one near the old tea garden."

Meghna nodded quickly. "You mean the one near the abandoned shrine? The one with all the vines growing over it?"

Kurchi's eyes lit up. "Yes. That must be it! The magical compass hasn't lit up yet, but maybe this riddle is like the last one—we don't need it to guide us this time."

The next morning, the girls packed early. Kurchi's father added some extra snacks and even handed them a small torchlight.

"Just in case it's darker than expected," he said with a wink. "Oh, and take my old compass too. You never know when magic gets moody."

Kurchi grinned. "Thanks, Baba."

The girls made their way through narrow lanes and muddy paths, past rusted fences and tangled bushes, until they reached the old tea garden. The grass was tall and wild, and the trees bent over the path like they were trying to hide it from view.

In the middle of the clearing stood the well.

It was made of grey stone, covered in moss and curling vines. Nearby, a stone plaque lay half-buried in the ground. Faded as it was, the girls could still see a lotus symbol carved on it.

Kurchi began to hum a gentle tune. The air felt thick with stillness. Slowly, the vines curled away from the rim of the well. The stones groaned, and something deep below stirred.

A whisper floated up—not words, but strange sounds. It didn't feel scary. Just very, very old. Like the sound of a memory.

Then the ground near the well cracked open. A round stone tunnel appeared, leading into the earth. Spiral stairs twisted down into the dark.

"This is becoming a habit," Meghna whispered, staring into the hole.

One by one, they climbed down.

Inside, the tunnel was quiet—too quiet. Their footsteps echoed for a bit, then even that sound faded away. The walls were lined with carvings, but no torches lit up like before. The air was thick, almost like it was holding its breath.

Finally, they reached a round chamber covered in soft white sand. In the center stood a stone pedestal. Behind it was a tall, dark mirror that didn't reflect anything at all.

Carved into the pedestal were these words:

"Only one voice shall open the way.

Only silence shall guide the day.

Those who speak shall lose their way."

Kurchi shivered. "So... we can't talk?" Meghna whispered.

Suddenly, the sand near her feet crumbled into a deep hole! Meghna jumped back, eyes wide.

"Okay! No talking!" she mouthed.

They all nodded and looked around. Three tunnels led away from the chamber. Above each one, white glowing runes changed and danced until they became shapes: a tree, a river, and a star.

Ghurni pointed to the shapes and then at the tunnels. She silently suggested they each take one path.

Kurchi hesitated. But then the mirror rippled.

Inside it, she saw herself—but older, braver, glowing with a gentle light. The older Kurchi smiled and nodded before fading away.

Kurchi felt calm.

She chose the river path. The tunnel was narrow and lined with small wind chimes—but they didn't make any sound. Instead, they just shimmered softly. At the end of the path, Kurchi entered a room filled with musical instruments made of stone—a flute, a drum, a veena.

Inside her mind, a voice whispered: "Sing without sound. Let the voice within guide you."

Kurchi picked up the flute and closed her eyes. She remembered the first song she ever sang when they opened the magical book. Though the flute made no sound, the air around her shimmered like water in sunlight. The room glowed gently.

Meanwhile, Ghurni was walking the path with the tree symbol. On her tunnel walls were riddles carved into the stone.

She read them carefully and answered in her head.

"The more you take, the more you leave behind."

Footsteps.

"I speak without a mouth and hear without ears."

An echo.

Each time she answered, the path lit up below her feet. At the end, she found a glowing orb floating in the air. She touched it and saw a vision—her younger self solving her first puzzle at school. She smiled and stepped forward.

Meghna's tunnel, marked with a star, led to a strange maze of rooms. In each room, there was an object: a marble, a ribbon, a photo.

They weren't random. The marble was Kurchi's from class two. The ribbon had belonged to Ghurni. The photo was from the school fair—all three of them, smiling.

Meghna carefully placed the objects on a stone pedestal in the order she remembered them.

A door opened soundlessly.

She stepped through and found herself back in the main chamber, where Ghurni and Kurchi were already waiting.

The tall mirror was glowing.

Then, it cracked down the middle and opened like a door.

Out stepped a tall figure, cloaked in smoke, holding a staff made of stone. His voice didn't come through his mouth—it echoed inside their minds.

"You have walked the path of silence," said the Echo Keeper. "You have sung without sound, solved without words, remembered without help. You are ready."

From the air above the pedestal, a new object floated down—a silver glass orb, glowing with soft starlight.

Meghna reached out and touched it.

Right then, the magical compass on Kurchi's chest glowed bright violet.

As they climbed out of the tunnel, Kurchi tried to hum—but for a moment, no sound came out.

Then it did.

Ghurni blinked. "Was that supposed to happen?"

Chapter 11
Shadows in the Vines

The next day, the morning didn't feel like a morning at all. The sky was thick with dark, gray clouds, and the sun was nowhere to be seen. The air was still, and everything seemed too quiet. Kurchi, Ghurni, and Meghna were sitting together in Kurchi's rooftop room, still buzzing with excitement from the strange events at the dried-up well the night before.

In the middle of the room, the silver orb lay silent and cool, no longer glowing. The magical compass, tucked away in Meghna's pocket, hadn't lit up since the night before.

Kurchi's father entered the room, carrying a tray with toasted bread, orange marmalade, and three cups of milk tea. "Eat well, girls," he said with his usual cheerful smile. "You'll need your strength."

Kurchi squinted at him. "Why do you always say things like that right before something weird happens?"

He just winked. "Just a father's intuition."

After he left, the three friends gathered around the Voicekeeper's Guide, which now lay open, but the pages were blank. It was strange because the guide usually had something to say, but today, there was nothing.

Suddenly, the orb began to glow faintly, casting silver shadows across the room. The pages of the guide flipped on their own, and words slowly appeared.

"Before the path of light may bloom,

One must pass through creeping gloom.

Where vines have swallowed time and stone,

The fire's path must walk alone."

Ghurni read the words aloud, her voice low with curiosity. "The fire's path...."

Kurchi frowned. "And 'where vines have swallowed time and stone'—that sounds like ruins."

Meghna clapped her hands excitedly. "I know exactly where! Remember the old stepwell near the fig trees by the hill past the station? It's all covered in vines now."

Kurchi stood up. "Then that's our next stop."

By late afternoon, the girls had reached the foot of the old hill. The path twisted and turned, tangled with mossy boulders and wild bushes that scraped their legs and clung to their clothes. They followed a broken trail of stone steps up toward what was left of an old temple, now mostly crumbled. Thick green vines had swallowed the building, covering everything like a heavy blanket. Forgotten statues of deities poked out from beneath layers of moss, looking like they were lost in time.

The stepwell was ahead, wide and empty, its ancient stones worn by years of weather and neglect. The air around it felt cooler, almost as if the ground beneath their feet was humming with energy.

"I think this is it," she whispered, her heart racing.

Suddenly, the air grew tense. A sharp hiss echoed through the silence, and the vines began to twist and move. The girls stepped back, startled, but instead of striking, the vines shaped themselves into a figure.

It looked like a woman, tall and graceful, her arms stretched wide. Her face was made of bark and leaves, and her eyes glowed a deep, eerie green.

"I am Vayana," the figure said in a voice that sounded like the rustling of leaves. "Guardian of the Forgotten Hill. Only the bearer of flame may pass. The others must wait."

Kurchi stepped forward, her heart pounding in her chest. “What do you mean?”

“The fire in your heart must face the darkness alone,” Vayana said. “Your voice will guide you. If you pass, the next key will be yours.”

Ghurni and Meghna exchanged worried looks. “No way,” Meghna said. “We’re not letting you go alone!”

But the vines rose around Kurchi, wrapping gently around her. Vayana’s voice came again, calm and firm. “This is her path. Yours will follow.”

Before Kurchi could say anything else, the vines pulled her downward into the stepwell.

Kurchi’s world twisted and swirled into complete silence. She blinked, and when her eyes opened again, she found herself standing in a strange version of the stepwell. The walls seemed alive, pulsing with light, like veins under skin. Violet fireflies floated around her, casting a soft, glowing light.

In front of her were three doors, each marked with a glowing symbol. One had a songbird, the second a mask, and the third had a mirror.

The Voice keeper's Guide appeared in her hands, its pages flipping on their own.

"Choose wisely. One voice is true. One voice is false. One voice is forgotten."

Kurchi bit her lip. "Okay," she whispered to herself. "Let's do this." She stepped toward the door with the songbird symbol.

Inside the door, Kurchi found herself in a round room filled with echoes. Her own voice floated around her, singing soft lullabies, old songs she had heard as a child, even ones she didn't recognize. The songs filled every corner of the room, and her voice seemed to dance with the walls.

Suddenly, a figure stepped out from the shadows. It looked just like Kurchi, but much older, with a stern expression on her face.

"Why do you sing?" the figure asked, her voice deep.

Kurchi blinked, confused. "To remember," she replied.

"And what if memory lies?" the figure asked again, her voice even colder. "What if your song is just noise?"

Kurchi stepped forward, her voice steady. "Then I will keep singing until I find the truth."

The figure smiled, and then vanished, leaving only the sound of Kurchi's voice echoing in the room. The walls cracked and crumbled around her, and she was back in the central chamber. Two doors faded away, leaving only the one with the mirror symbol.

Kurchi stepped through it.

She found herself standing in a room filled with floating candles. The warm light from the flames reflected in the mirror that hung in front of her. In the center of the room, a single large flame hovered above a silver stand.

As she approached, the flame flickered and shifted. First, it took the shape of her mother and father, then transformed into the faces of Ghurni and Meghna, before finally becoming her own face, staring back at her from the flames.

"You are the Voicekeeper," the flame whispered, its voice soft and ancient. "But even your voice must know silence. To lead, you must first listen."

Kurchi closed her eyes. She didn't sing. Instead, she just listened to the quiet, letting the silence fill her. Then, deep beneath the ground, she heard it—a faint, far-off note, like a seed cracking open.

Kurchi sang—not with her voice, but from her heart. The flame burst into golden light, filling the room with warmth and light.

Back at the surface, the vines slowly unraveled themselves. The guardian, Vayana, nodded. "She has passed."

Kurchi was pulled back up from the stepwell. In her hand, she held a carved wooden flute.

"A Voicekeeper's gift," Vayana explained. "Each bearer earns her instrument. The next path lies to the east. Beneath the earth. Beyond memory."

The guardian melted back into the vines, and everything returned to stillness.

The girls stood in silence for a moment, taking it all in.

Meghna was the first to speak. “That. Was. So. Cool.”

Kurchi managed a faint smile. “And terrifying.”

When they got back home, Kurchi’s compass finally glowed again. The arrow pointed firmly toward the east.

As they sat together under the darkening sky, Kurchi found herself staring up at the first few stars peeking through the clouds.

The old words from the basin returned to her mind — the strange prophecy they had once read aloud but not fully understood.

"When the Voices grow silent..."

She touched her throat lightly, remembering the way her voice had called the library awake, the way it had shaped the fire tonight.

“What if the prophecy was about us all along?” Kurchi said softly.

Ghurni, fiddling with the brass key they had found earlier, shrugged. “Maybe. Or maybe we’re just part of a bigger story.”

Meghna yawned and leaned back against the wall. “Either way, we’re in it now.”

Chapter 12
Through The Tunnel Beneath Time

The night still hung heavy in the air when Kurchi, Ghurni, and Meghna gathered again in their rooftop room.

None of them had spoken much since returning from the stepwell.

The memory of the prophecy they had once read — the one about three who must rise — lingered between them like a soft, invisible thread.

The stars twinkled above the suburban rooftops, and the night air smelled like earth and flowers from the nearby shiuli trees.

As usual, Kurchi's father brought them a treat: steamed sandesh and warm milk with cardamom.

"You'll need your strength," he said, giving them a wink before disappearing.

Kurchi picked up her wooden flute, which she had earned from the stepwell trial, and played a soft note. It echoed strangely, making the room feel deeper.

The Voicekeeper's Guide fluttered its pages on its own. Soon, a sketch appeared—lines and shadows that turned into a picture of a brick-lined tunnel with glowing moss. Above it, the words "The Tunnel Beneath Time" appeared. Beneath that, a riddle began to form:

"Where silence hums and pasts reside,

Beneath the banyan's crooked pride,

Through hollow roots and ancient rhyme,

Lies the tunnel beneath all time."

Ghurni leaned in. "It's giving us another riddle and map."

Meghna pointed at the sketch. “That looks like the banyan tree near the railway line. You know, the one that leans like it’s whispering to the tracks?”

Kurchi nodded. “Let’s go first thing in the morning.”

The next morning, the trio set out at sunrise. They packed their backpacks with torches, rope, snacks, and their magical compass, and made their way through narrow lanes and over railway tracks to the old banyan tree.

Its roots were twisted, curling like fingers around the earth. Its trunk was hollowed out, dark with age, and one massive root had even lifted a stone platform. They walked around the tree until Meghna shouted, “Here!”

A patch of moss near the base of the tree was glowing faintly. Ghurni brushed it aside and found a carved symbol beneath: a treble clef, an eye, and a flame—the same symbols from the pedestal in the library.

Kurchi placed her hand over the symbol.

The ground rumbled, and with a soft groan, the earth beneath the tree split open, revealing a spiral staircase leading down into darkness.

They lit their torches and started their descent. The staircase was narrow and damp, with carvings on the walls of children, owls, books, and stars. The air grew cooler as they went deeper, and a strange hum seemed to echo through the stones.

At the bottom, they entered a large underground tunnel made of red bricks, with moss growing between them.

Faded murals on the walls showed children holding lanterns and walking through ancient lands.

“This has to be some kind of time tunnel,” Meghna whispered.

Kurchi nodded. “Let’s keep going. The compass is pointing straight ahead.”

As they walked, the tunnel shimmered slightly, and images began to appear in the air, like misty memories. They saw a boy with a flute leading villagers through a storm. A girl whose glowing hands lit a dark cave filled with wolves. A child solving riddles to lift a curse from an old temple.

“These must be the ones who came before us,” Ghurni said softly.

“Maybe... our earlier selves?” Meghna added.

Kurchi stepped closer to one of the visions. “Or the guardians we’re meant to become.”

The visions faded, leaving behind a warm feeling—as though the tunnel itself was blessing them.

At the end of the tunnel, they found a large stone door, round and smooth, with no handles or hinges. Just a row of strange symbols: musical notes, puzzle shapes, and stars.

The Voicekeeper’s Guide flipped open again.

“Three voices must speak as one.

One of song, one of riddle, one of memory.

The right harmony will unlock the way.”

Kurchi took out her flute and played a short melody—one her father used to hum.

Ghurni thought for a moment, then recited a riddle she remembered from their visit to the library:

"What walks forward but looks behind?

Its face reflects, but its feet unwind."

Meghna didn't hesitate. "Diya. Our classmate. She gave me her notebook when I forgot mine last week. She didn't even ask why."

The symbols on the door began to glow. A deep, resonant hum filled the tunnel, and slowly, the stone door creaked open.

Beyond the door was a circular chamber with a dome ceiling covered in tiny glowing dots, like stars. In the center was a pedestal made of clear crystal, and above it hovered a glowing sphere, pale blue like a frozen star.

Ghurni whispered, "It's a memory-stone."

As Kurchi stepped forward, the orb flickered, and a new vision appeared in the air. It showed a library burning, its shelves collapsing. Voices screamed. Then three children—one with a glowing hand, one with a flute, and one with a book—stood before the flames. The fire froze.

Then everything went dark. A single sentence appeared above the orb:

"What has been once forgotten must again be remembered."

As the orb faded, part of the wall shimmered, revealing a secret door. Beyond it was a narrow passage filled with cobwebs and vines.

The compass shifted, pointing in a new direction. The Voicekeeper's Guide flipped to a fresh page with a new message:

"The trials continue. One light has been restored. The second lies where moonlight does not reach."

Ghurni made a note. "That sounds like a cave."

Meghna yawned. "One thing at a time. Let's go back first."

Kurchi nodded, though her heart was racing. The vision of the burning library felt urgent—like a memory trying to break free.

By the time they emerged from the banyan tree, the sun was setting. The roots of the tree slowly closed up, hiding the tunnel once more.

Chapter 13
The Cave That Hummed

The following morning arrived with a soft drizzle, and the air was filled with the smell of petrichor and champa blossoms. At Kurchi's home, the rooftop room buzzed with quiet energy as the girls gathered, still thinking about the memory-stone they had discovered under the banyan tree.

Kurchi sat cross-legged with the Voicekeeper's Guide open before her. The pages had changed again overnight, revealing a drawing of a crescent-shaped cave mouth, surrounded by tall grass and shaded by massive sal trees. Above it was scrawled:

"Where moonlight does not reach,

yet the earth sings in echoes deep.

Find the stone where silence meets sound."

Ghurni pulled out a map of their neighborhood and the surrounding areas that she'd copied from Kurchi's father's old atlas. "There's a dense patch of forest just past the old irrigation canal. No one really goes there—it's too wild."

Meghna looked up from polishing the compass, which now pulsed in short beats. "Then that's where we're going."

Just then, Kurchi's father peeked into the room. "Planning another little trip, are you?" he asked, balancing a tray of roasted muri, chopped cucumber, and lime.

Ghurni nodded. "To the forest this time."

"Ah," he said with a twinkle in his eye, placing the tray on the table. "Don't forget the west side of the forest has a cave that was once used by traveling fakirs during the rainy season. Locals say it hums during storms."

Kurchi raised an eyebrow. "How do you know all this?"

He grinned. "History, myths, and puzzles remember everything—even when people don't."

By noon, the rain had cleared and the girls were on their way, dressed in rainboots and jackets, carrying torches, snacks, a notebook, and their magical tools.

They entered the forest from the western edge, pushing aside tall elephant grass and ducking under low branches. Birds chirped overhead, and a mongoose darted across their path.

"Look," Meghna said, pointing at a tree marked with the same symbol from the pedestal: treble clef, eye, and flame—scratched faintly into the bark.

Following the symbols carved onto trees and rocks, they made their way to a shaded clearing where the ground dipped slightly. There, half-hidden under moss and ferns, was a low, dark cave mouth, shaped like a sideways crescent.

The entrance shimmered faintly.

"It's real," Kurchi whispered.

They stepped inside, their torches casting long shadows on damp walls. At first, it was silent except for the crunch of their footsteps on the rocky floor. Then, they heard it: a low hum, deep and constant, like the earth itself was singing.

Kurchi walked to the center of the cave and hummed softly. Her voice merged with the hum perfectly, and the walls began to glow with lines of light—revealing etched symbols and ancient writing all around them.

Ghurni stepped closer and began reading aloud, deciphering bits and pieces: "When the voice aligns, and memory meets truth, the path to the keeper will open…"

A soft click echoed.

A hidden section of the wall slid open, revealing a tunnel shaped like a spiral shell, with steps leading deeper into the earth.

They descended cautiously, entering a wide cavern lit by blue fireflies trapped in hanging crystals. In the center stood three stone platforms, each carved with a symbol: a flame, a treble clef, and an eye.

A whispering voice filled the air—more felt than heard.

"To pass, each must offer their strength.

Voice. Memory. Insight.

And answer what binds the forgotten to the now."

The girls exchanged looks and took their places. Kurchi stood on the treble clef, Ghurni on the eye, Meghna on the flame.

Then, from the ceiling, visions dropped like water droplets into shimmering pools—each showing forgotten moments from their own lives: small, unimportant acts of kindness, unnoticed bravery, times when they chose truth over ease.

"I remember this," Meghna said softly. "I helped that puppy out of the drain and didn't tell anyone."

Ghurni nodded. "And I told Me that I had copied homework once… even when I knew it'd get me into trouble."

Kurchi added, "I gave up singing for a whole year when Mum got sick. I didn't want her to feel sad."

The pools stilled. The air thickened with warmth.

"To remember what matters… is to begin."

The center of the chamber split open, revealing a second orb—darker than the last, with flecks of gold swirling inside it.

As Kurchi reached for it, the orb dissolved into the Voicekeeper's Guide, merging into the pages and lighting up a whole new section.

The book now showed a map—new paths, previously invisible, now revealed. One led to the riverbed ruins. Another pointed to a windmill hill outside the town.

More riddles filled the pages.

At the bottom of the page was a new inscription:

"Two lights now burn.

One remains buried beneath the stone of names."

"Stone of names?" Ghurni said, eyebrows raised.

"Maybe an old graveyard?" Meghna guessed.

"Or an abandoned monument," Kurchi added. "We'll find it."

Just then, the ground shook slightly—a distant rumble. The humming stopped.

And the tunnel entrance behind them began to collapse.

They ran—dodging falling stones, ducking through the now-flickering cave corridor. The humming had turned into a groan.

Kurchi led with the compass glowing steadily in her hand. Ghurni carried the book. Meghna kept calling out the directions she remembered from the spiral chamber.

As they reached the mouth of the cave, the final rock crashed behind them, sealing the passage.

They lay there, panting in the clearing.

Kurchi looked up at the sky. “We made it.”

Ghurni smiled. “Barely.”

Meghna grinned. “That’s what makes it an adventure.”

Chapter 14
The Stone of Names

It had rained all night, and by morning, the sky was a patchwork of drifting clouds and soft sunlight. Kurchi was already on the rooftop, flipping through the Voicekeeper's Guide, which now gleamed faintly with the two collected orbs embedded in its center. Ghurni arrived first, her notebook bulging with scribbled clues. Meghna followed close behind, clutching a faded envelope she'd found in her family's storage trunk—an old letter from her great-grandfather mentioning a stone memorial with names carved in a spiral.

"That might be our 'Stone of Names'," she said, placing the envelope beside the glowing book. "It's in the outskirts of the old burial ground—near the banyan grove where no one goes anymore."

Kurchi's father entered with a large tray: toast with mango pickle, boiled eggs, and glasses of nimbu soda fizzing with sugar crystals.

"Stone of Names, you say?" he asked, setting the tray down. "There's an old tale of a grave marker with shifting names on it. Every full moon, the names change—some vanish, others appear."

"Real or just a ghost story?" Ghurni asked.

He shrugged, smiling. "Many ghost stories are just histories forgotten."

Kurchi traced the path on their map. "Let's find out."

After lunch, they ventured out, wearing jeans, caps, and scarves. As they neared the banyan grove, the sounds of the town grew faint behind them. Wind rustled the dry grass. Crows flew in slow, wide circles overhead. At the center of the grove, partially hidden by undergrowth, stood an oval stone, taller than Kurchi, weathered and moss-covered. At first glance, it looked plain. But then the compass buzzed.

The girls stepped closer. Names began to shimmer faintly on the stone's surface—written in various languages and scripts, glowing softly in the midday shade.

"It's responding to us," whispered Ghurni.

Kurchi stepped forward and sang the first line of an old village song —one her mother used to hum. The names rearranged themselves. At the very top of the stone, three names floated in glowing script: Kurchi, Meghna, Ghurni.

Meghna gasped. "We're part of this…"

The moment their names appeared, the ground beneath the stone trembled. A circular platform rose from the earth, bearing a small, cracked hourglass and three marble spheres, each etched with a symbol: a spiral, a flame, and a crescent moon. A stone guardian emerged—its face blank, its eyes glowing.

"To hold the light, You must pass through shadow. Solve the names forgotten, And time shall guide you."

Ghurni knelt by the hourglass. "This is a time-based riddle." The book fluttered open beside her, revealing three riddles:

I disappear the moment you say my name.

I speak without a mouth and hear without ears.

I am not alive, but I grow; I don't have lungs, but I need air.

"Silence," Ghurni said, "Echo… and Fire!"

As she called out the last answer, the three spheres glowed and began to levitate. The hourglass flipped, and grains of glowing sand trickled down. Then, the platform split apart, revealing a stone casket nestled in a pit, containing the third orb, brighter than the others and pulsing with color.

Kurchi lifted it, and it dissolved into the book—fusing with the others.

With all three orbs in place, the Voicekeeper's Guide began to hum, just like the cave. Lines of golden ink raced across the pages, drawing intricate maps, glyphs, and phrases. At the center of a new page, a symbol formed—a circle of three, with their initials surrounding an ancient glyph. Below it, a sentence began to write itself:

The Library is open to you. But beware, for others seek its light. And not all who read… remember.

The compass snapped shut with a loud click, then slowly reopened—revealing a new needle, pointing not to north, but toward the mountain temple drawn on the last page.

As the girls packed up to leave, they heard something in the trees—a rustle, but no wind. A figure stood beyond the grove's edge. It wore a dark cloak and held an object that glimmered like the Voicekeeper's Guide—but blackened, broken. The figure didn't speak. But when Kurchi stepped forward, the figure slowly mimicked her humming, only it sounded… wrong. Twisted.

They all stepped back. The figure vanished behind a shimmer of light, like mist swallowed by sunlight.

Meghna clutched Kurchi's arm. "Who—what—was that?"

Ghurni whispered, "I think… someone else has a book like ours."

Kurchi closed the Voicekeeper's Guide carefully. "Then we're not the only ones reading these stories."

The girls returned quietly, minds full of questions. Outside, the sky turned copper as the sun dipped below the clouds. The wind carried the scent of wet leaves and something ancient. Kurchi opened the book again.

Next: The Temple of the Shifting Wind.

She looked up at her friends. "We're not just guarding a book."

Ghurni nodded. "We're guarding its memory."

Meghna smiled, eyes gleaming. "Then let's remember everything."

Chapter 15
The Temple of the Shifting Wind

The next morning arrived with a crisp, cool breeze carrying the scent of the distant mountains. Kurchi sat cross-legged on the rooftop, her hands resting on the now-closed Voicekeeper's Guide. The glowing orbs within the book pulsed softly, as though calling her to follow them. Her father was in the kitchen, humming a tune as he flipped through an old history book about forgotten temples. She had been waiting for Meghna and Ghurni to arrive, eager to share the news of what they had learned the previous day.

A soft knock on the door brought Kurchi out of her reverie. Ghurni and Meghna stepped onto the rooftop, their faces set with determination.

"Ready for another adventure?" Ghurni asked, her eyes bright with excitement.

Meghna nodded eagerly. "I've been thinking about the temple all night. What do you think it looks like?"

Kurchi held up the Voicekeeper's Guide. "I'm not sure, but the book says it's somewhere near the Temple of the Shifting Wind. We have to follow the compass again. This time, it will guide us to the temple where the real challenge begins."

Kurchi's father emerged from the kitchen, wiping his hands on a towel. He set down the book he'd been reading and smiled warmly at the girls. "I have something for you," he said, reaching into his pocket. He pulled out a small leather pouch and handed it to Kurchi. "It's filled with dried herbs—just in case you need them for a quick energy boost. I also added a bit of cinnamon, in case you get too tired. And take these," he added, holding up a few small silver pendants. “These will help protect you from magic that tries to interfere with your minds. Wear them around your neck, close to your skin.”

Kurchi’s father always knew how to make them feel prepared. Meghna and Ghurni nodded in gratitude as Kurchi tucked the pouch into her bag and hung the pendants around their necks.

“Thank you, Uncle,” Ghurni said.

With everything packed, the girls stepped out of the rooftop room. The air was cooler now, and the sky shimmered with the faint glow of the rising sun. They didn’t need to speak; the excitement was written on their faces. They knew this next journey was more than just another puzzle or riddle—it was something much bigger.

The Voicekeeper’s Guide pulsed gently as they followed the compass’s needle, which now pointed towards the distant Temple of the Shifting Wind. The path was winding, cutting through dense forests and crossing narrow rivers. They passed villages and hills, the landscape growing more rugged with each step. As they traveled, Kurchi couldn’t help but feel the weight of the book and the mysterious force pulling them onward.

By the time they reached the base of the mountain where the temple was supposed to be, the sun was high, casting long shadows over the rocky cliffs. They stopped to rest by a spring, the water clear and cold. As they sat down, Kurchi opened the book once more. It shimmered with golden light, revealing a new clue:

The Temple is not what it seems,

Beneath the wind, a hidden stream.

Find the heart where the breeze spins,

And you will see where it begins.

“The breeze…” Ghurni muttered. “It says we need to follow it, but how do we know where it spins?”

Kurchi bit her lip, flipping through the pages of the book. The compass still pointed upward, its needle unwavering.

“I think it means the wind is part of the temple itself,” Meghna said slowly. “It’s not just a place; it’s connected to something we’ll have to find first. It could be the way the temple shifts.”

Kurchi closed the book with a quiet snap. "Then we need to keep going."

The climb up the mountain was steep and difficult, but they were determined. The landscape grew more mysterious as they ascended. There were no trees now—only sharp rock formations and narrow crevices where the wind howled through like a ghostly whisper.

Suddenly, the sound of a whistle broke through the wind, followed by the distinct hum of a soft melody. Kurchi froze, listening. It was faint but undeniable. The wind carried it, like a song, though there was no one around to sing it.

“That’s not from the mountain,” Kurchi whispered, her heart racing.

“It’s coming from inside the temple,” Ghurni replied. “We’re close.”

The girls quickened their pace, the wind beginning to howl around them as if urging them to hurry.

After hours of climbing, they finally reached a plateau. At the far end, hidden behind a veil of thick mist, was the entrance to the Temple of the Shifting Wind. The temple looked ancient, its structure made of gray stone and ivy, its towering spires reaching up to the sky like fingers outstretched in silent prayer. A heavy mist swirled around it, giving the place an ethereal, almost dreamlike quality.

“There’s no door,” Meghna murmured, stepping forward cautiously.

Kurchi noticed the ground around the temple was covered in strange symbols—swirls, spirals, and jagged lines, as if the wind had etched them into the earth itself. Ghurni bent down to touch one of the markings. As her fingers brushed the symbol, the stone beneath them rumbled, and the mist parted like curtains.

The temple revealed its true form: a large circular courtyard with three stone pillars at its center, each carved with intricate symbols matching those on the ground. At the top of each pillar was an empty space—like an offering bowl—but nothing filled it.

“It’s like a puzzle,” Kurchi said, her voice barely above a whisper.

“We need to fill these bowls,” Meghna said, already searching for something.

A gust of wind swept through the courtyard, stirring the mist and making the stone pillars seem to shimmer. Ghurni stood still, her brow furrowed in concentration.

"The book says we must follow the breeze. But how do we catch it?"

Kurchi held out the Voicekeeper's Guide and looked closely at the image of the stone pillars. One of the pages glowed faintly, showing three items—the wind crystal, a songbird's feather, and a stone that hums.

"I think we need these items to complete the puzzle," Kurchi said. "The wind crystal could be hidden in the temple, the feather could be linked to the wind's song, and the humming stone… we might already have it."

Meghna glanced at Kurchi's hand. "You're right. The humming stone is the orb, isn't it?"

Kurchi nodded. "We'll need to find the other two."

As they stepped forward, the wind picked up once again, this time guiding them toward an opening in the temple's wall.

"We have to go inside," Kurchi said, her voice firm with resolve.

The girls made their way into the temple, the sound of wind echoing all around them, as if the very air itself was calling them deeper into the mystery.

Inside, the temple was vast—stone corridors led to multiple chambers, each filled with strange carvings, pools of water, and floating lanterns. The air was thick with an ancient energy that made the hairs on the back of their necks stand on end. In the center of one large hall stood a massive stone door, covered in intricate carvings.

At its base was a single small, circular pedestal, on which rested a shimmering blue crystal.

“This must be the wind crystal,” Meghna said, her voice a mix of awe and fear.

Kurchi stepped forward, but the moment she touched the pedestal, a gust of wind blew from behind them, slamming the stone door shut. A booming voice echoed through the hall.

To claim the wind,

You must pass the test—

Speak with the earth,

And the sky shall open.

Ghurni took a step back, her mind racing. “What does that mean? Speak with the earth?”

Kurchi stood still, remembering the symbols outside the temple—the spirals, the swirls. It had to be a riddle, and they needed to solve it quickly.

“We have to speak the language of the earth and the wind,” Kurchi said, her voice steady. “Let’s work together.”

As they stood before the stone door, the riddle began to take shape in their minds. The earth… and the sky.

Chapter 16
The Whispering Winds

The stone door loomed in front of them, its surface covered in strange, swirling symbols. A faint hum of wind circled around them, its soft breeze tugging at their clothes as if urging them forward. Kurchi, Ghurni, and Meghna stood in tense silence, the riddle from the Voicekeeper's Guide hanging between them like an invisible weight.

"To claim the wind," Kurchi murmured, reading the riddle once more in her mind. "You must pass the test—speak with the earth, and the sky shall open."

Meghna furrowed her brow, frustration evident in her voice. "What does that even mean? How are we supposed to speak with the earth and the sky?"

She pressed her fingers against the cool stone of the pedestal, her mind racing for any hidden clues beneath its surface, but the stone remained silent. Ghurni, however, had already begun to scan the carvings around them. She traced her fingers along the swirling patterns, her sharp eyes narrowing with concentration.

“There’s something familiar about these symbols,” she said quietly. “They’re not just decorations. I think they might represent something—elements, perhaps. The earth and the sky.”

Kurchi paced back and forth, her thoughts swirling. “The earth… and the sky,” she muttered. “We’ve seen these symbols before. They’re everywhere.”

She stopped in front of one of the larger symbols, a spiral that seemed to mimic a whirlwind. “This is the wind,” Kurchi said, pointing to the pattern. “The wind’s connected to both the earth and the sky in some way. Maybe the answer is in how they both interact."

Ghurni paused beside her, her eyes lighting up as she recalled something. "Wait a minute… remember the story my parents told me? The one about the ancient winds? They said that long ago, the earth and the sky communicated through the elements. Earth would speak through the mountains and valleys, while the sky would answer with windstorms or clear skies. The language was in the patterns they created—storms, whirlwinds, the way the clouds moved."

Meghna's eyes widened with realization. "So, we have to speak the language of the wind and the earth to open the door? We have to listen to them first?"

Kurchi nodded slowly. "Exactly. The wind and the earth are in constant conversation. We just have to figure out how to listen—and then how to speak back."

The girls settled in front of the stone door, the swirling carvings surrounding them like an intricate web. Kurchi closed her eyes, reaching out with all her senses. She focused on the hum of the wind, the rustling leaves, the subtle sound of nature's rhythm. Slowly, she reached out her hand to touch the stone, and a shiver ran down her spine. The wind seemed to respond to her touch, swirling around her fingertips like a gentle caress.

"I think the earth wants us to understand the language of the wind," Kurchi said quietly, as if the wind itself had whispered the answer to her. "We need to listen to it."

Ghurni crouched beside the pedestal, her fingers tracing the base of the stone. She stopped at a small groove, barely visible in the dim light, almost hidden by the shadows. It was a thin line carved into the stone, almost as if something sharp had marked it. Ghurni's eyes sparkled as she uncovered more symbols hidden beneath the grime of centuries.

"There's something here," she said, her voice tinged with excitement. "A hidden inscription. This must be the key."

Kurchi leaned in closer, squinting at the markings. They weren't like the other symbols—these were simple, straight lines, intersected by short diagonal cuts.

"This looks like…" Kurchi murmured, her heart racing as she recognized the pattern. "Wind patterns. It's the wind's language."

"That's it!" Meghna exclaimed, her face lighting up. "These lines are meant to represent the way the wind flows! We need to recreate the pattern in the air."

Kurchi's heart raced. "I know the wind is part of our powers. I just need to focus."

She took a deep breath, her fingers still resting on the stone. Then, slowly, she raised her hand toward the sky, and the wind seemed to shift in response. A gentle breeze wrapped around her fingertips, picking up speed, swirling through the air like a dancer finding its rhythm. The girls stood still, feeling the wind speak to them, each gust and swirl a message they were beginning to understand.

Ghurni watched her closely, a thoughtful expression on her face. "I think… you need to sing to it, Kurchi. Your voice. The way you control the elements. Maybe the wind can't understand us without your song."

Kurchi hesitated for a moment, her breath caught in her chest. She felt the hum of the Voicekeeper's Guide against her skin, urging her to act. She took a deep breath and began to sing. At first, her voice was soft, uncertain, but as the melody grew stronger, the wind responded. It whipped through the stones, swirling in patterns that mirrored the lines Ghurni had uncovered.

The song was slow, haunting, and the Voicekeeper's Guide pulsed along with her voice, guiding her. The air seemed to shimmer with the energy of the song, and Kurchi's voice filled the temple, rising and falling like the gentle sway of trees in the wind.

As the final note echoed through the temple, the stone pedestal hummed beneath her fingers. The symbols around them shifted, their edges beginning to swirl and twist together in a mesmerizing dance. The wind surged again, this time with purpose, and the stone door creaked open, its heavy weight lifting with a groan.

The girls stood in awe as the massive door slowly parted, revealing a dark hallway beyond. The air felt cool, and the faint scent of ancient incense lingered in the air, as if the temple had been waiting for them to unlock its secrets for centuries.

"Good job, Kurchi," Ghurni said, her voice full of admiration. "Your song worked. I can't believe it."

Kurchi smiled, still feeling the reverberations of her voice in the air, the wind swirling around them in appreciation.

"I didn't know it would work like that. I guess it's more than just magic—it's about listening."

Meghna, her eyes sparkling with determination, stepped forward. "We're not done yet. Let's see what's inside."

The girls carefully entered the hallway, their footsteps muffled by the thick carpet of dust beneath their feet. They moved cautiously, unsure of what awaited them. As they neared the end of the hall, they saw another pedestal bathed in a faint, ethereal glow. On the pedestal sat an object—a small wind crystal, shimmering with an inner light that pulsed softly with energy.

Kurchi approached it slowly, the book in her hands urging her forward. As her fingers brushed the crystal, a melodic hum filled the air, one that seemed to resonate deep within her chest. It was as though the crystal itself was singing a song—a song that Kurchi could almost hear in her mind.

"This is it," Kurchi whispered, a sense of triumph rising within her. "The first part of the puzzle. We found it."

Ghurni stepped closer, her fingers grazing the surface of the pedestal. "Now we need the next piece."

The wind swirled around them once again, whispering through the temple as if in agreement. The girls exchanged a glance, their determination clear.

Chapter 17
The Trial of the Heart stone

The air felt alive around the girls as they stood before the glowing Wind Crystal, a stone that seemed to hum with energy. The whispers of the temple seemed to call to them, urging them to touch the shimmering crystal. Kurchi stepped forward, her fingers brushing its smooth surface. As soon as she touched it, a warm hum filled her chest, making her feel connected to the crystal in a strange, almost magical way.

"Do you think this is part of the puzzle?" Meghna asked, her voice filled with wonder.

"I think it is," Kurchi replied, her voice steady but full of awe. "This crystal… it feels like it's alive."

The crystal's glow grew brighter, swirling with colors that shifted in the air like a dance of light. A gust of wind blew through the temple, and the girls stepped back in surprise. The stone pedestal beneath their feet rumbled, and the wind crystal pulsed with a rhythm that seemed to echo inside them.

"It's responding to something," Ghurni said, her eyes darting around the room. "But to what?"

Suddenly, the walls of the temple began to shift. The carvings on the stones rearranged themselves, like ancient secrets unlocking. A large, ornate door, hidden in shadows, slowly creaked open with a sound that seemed both eerie and inviting.

Kurchi's heart raced. "The next step of the journey," she whispered, stepping toward the door. "Let's see what's beyond it."

The door led them into a massive chamber. It was like a small hall, with columns towering above them, reaching up toward the ceiling. The walls were decorated with beautiful frescoes of ancient guardians, their eyes glowing with a soft, ethereal light. In the center of the room, a large pedestal held a dark, heart-shaped gemstone—smooth and as black as the night sky.

"The Heartstone," Kurchi said, recognizing it from the stories her father had told her. "This is what we were looking for."

The girls slowly approached the pedestal, their steps echoing in the empty room. The Heartstone seemed to glow from within, casting long, eerie shadows on the walls. As Kurchi reached out to touch it, the air around them grew colder, and the space felt heavier, as if the entire room was holding its breath.

Ghurni frowned. "Are you sure we should touch it? The stories I've heard say only those with pure hearts can handle the Heartstone."

Kurchi hesitated for a moment, but something inside her pushed her forward. "We don't have a choice," she said quietly. "We have to see what happens."

She placed her hand on the Heartstone. As soon as her fingers touched its smooth surface, the room trembled. The Heartstone's glow intensified, filling the space with blinding light. Suddenly, the floor beneath them cracked open with a loud, terrifying noise.

The girls jumped back in shock as the ground split, revealing a dark chasm below. Dark winds swirled from the abyss, and the air was filled with soft, whispering voices.

"What’s happening?!" Meghna cried, panic rising in her voice.

"Stay calm!" Ghurni shouted, grabbing Meghna's arm. "This is part of the trial. We need to stay focused."

The wind howled louder, and Kurchi felt her heart race faster. "I can feel it," she said, her voice shaky. "The Heartstone is testing us. It’s testing our will."

The Heartstone’s glow shifted from dark black to a bright, brilliant white. It pulsed in a steady rhythm, like a heartbeat. Kurchi, still holding the stone, closed her eyes and focused all her energy on it.

"I think we have to listen to it," she said. "The Heartstone… it’s alive, and it’s speaking to us."

The winds grew louder, trying to drown her out, but Kurchi’s connection to the Heartstone deepened. She heard its words clearly in her mind.

"To prove your worth, you must face the trial. The Heartstone will test your strength, your resolve, and your unity. Only those who pass the test may proceed."

The wind howled once more, but this time, Kurchi didn’t flinch. She stood tall, her hand still pressed against the Heartstone. "We’re ready," she said, her voice steady. "We’ve come this far together. We won’t back down now."

The Heartstone responded, its light flickering like a heartbeat. Then, in a sudden burst of energy, the room seemed to freeze. The winds died down, and the chasm below them sealed with a deep rumble. The pedestal holding the Heartstone slowly began to rise until it was level with the girls. The glowing stone hovered in midair, surrounded by a shimmering aura.

"The trial begins now," Kurchi said, her voice strong as she turned to face her friends. "We need to solve the riddle. Together."

The room was silent for a moment, and then a deep, booming voice filled the air.

" The first test is one of trust. You must each walk alone, guided only by your heart. Face not what threatens you—but what weighs you down."

The ground trembled slightly, and suddenly the girls were no longer standing together.

Each was alone—isolated in a strange, shifting space that felt almost dreamlike.

There was no enemy to fight, no monster to escape—only the ache of loneliness and the cold voice of doubt whispering from the shadows.

Kurchi found herself standing on an endless plain, under a pale, empty sky. There were no paths, no landmarks—only the soft hum of the Heartstone, somewhere far ahead.

A memory played before her: her father, sitting by the window, looking tired and old. He was waiting for her to come home, calling out her name softly.

Kurchi's chest tightened. A voice inside whispered:

"You are not strong enough to protect the ones you love. You will fail them."

The more she walked toward her father's fading figure, the farther he seemed to drift away.

Tears stung her eyes, but she stopped running.

She closed her eyes and placed her hand over her heart.

"I can't carry every burden. But I can stand by them. I can believe in myself."

The plain brightened, the sky lifted, and her father's image gave her a nod of silent pride.

Kurchi stepped forward, the Heartstone's hum growing stronger.

Ghurni's world had turned into a dark maze—walls of endless mirrors surrounded her, each one showing her worst fears: failure, mistakes, letting everyone down.

Each reflection whispered:

"You will never solve the puzzle. You will lose everyone because you are not enough."

She stumbled from mirror to mirror, trying to escape the accusing faces.

Finally, she fell to her knees and covered her ears.

"I don't have to have all the answers," she whispered.

"I just have to keep trying, together with my friends."

The mirrors cracked and fell away, revealing a path of soft golden light leading her forward.

Meghna floated in a heavy, endless mist. Familiar voices echoed faintly—her parents calling her, their voices laced with sadness.

A distant vision appeared: her home, empty and silent without her. Guilt wrapped around her like heavy chains.

"You abandoned them. You chose adventure over love," the mist whispered.

Tears streamed down Meghna's face.

She pressed her palms together and spoke aloud, her voice trembling:

"I love them. I miss them. And when this journey is over, I'll return stronger and braver—for them."

The mist lightened, and a path opened through the fog, leading her back toward the Heartstone's glow.

As the girls each stepped through their separate trials, the chamber around them came back into focus. The Heartstone's light, once harsh and judging, now shone with a warm, steady glow.

A deep voice resonated in the air:

"The trial is complete. You have proven your worth. You are the new guardians. The path forward is open to you."

A beam of light shot out from the Heartstone, illuminating a hidden doorway in the room. The girls, exhausted but victorious, stood side by side. They had faced their fears and emerged stronger.

"We did it," Kurchi whispered, smiling at her friends. "Together."

Ghurni smiled. "I knew we could."

Meghna let out a deep breath. "We’re ready for whatever comes next."

Chapter 18
The Hidden Paths

The soft glow of the Heartstone faded, and the last echoes of the deep, resonant voice that had guided them through the trials still seemed to linger in the air. Kurchi, Ghurni, and Meghna stood at the edge of a newly revealed doorway, feeling the weight of what they had just experienced. The dark, heavy chamber now felt strangely calm, and the stone walls seemed to whisper ancient secrets.

Kurchi stepped forward first, reaching out to touch the door. The air around it shimmered like liquid light, unlike anything she had ever seen. For a moment, she hesitated, feeling both excited and nervous. Her heart raced.

“We’ve come so far,” she whispered to herself, her voice soft.

Ghurni, always the one to think things through, stood a little behind her, studying the door closely. “It feels... strange. Like this door wasn’t meant to open just yet,” she said, running her fingers along the smooth surface. It was warm to the touch, but there was a coldness hidden underneath, like fire and ice balanced together.

Meghna, who had been lost in her thoughts, finally spoke up. “Do you think we’re ready for whatever’s next?” she asked, her voice full of wonder and a little bit of fear.

Kurchi turned to her friends, her eyes filled with determination. “We’ve faced so much already. I think we’re ready.”

Her words hung in the air, and all three girls felt the truth of them. They had proven themselves by passing the trials, standing together through every challenge. Now, they were about to step into the next mystery, one that would bring them closer to uncovering the secrets of their powers—and whatever forces were behind the mysterious library.

Without another word, Kurchi pushed the door open. The threshold glowed brighter, revealing a narrow passageway, lit by soft golden lights embedded into the walls. The air smelled fresh, as if the room they had just left had been sealed off from the outside world for centuries. The floor was smooth stone, worn down by time.

The girls stepped into the corridor cautiously, their footsteps echoing in the silence. The walls, adorned with ancient carvings, felt oddly comforting, as if they had been waiting for them to arrive.

Meghna glanced around, feeling the strange weight of anticipation. "Where do you think this leads?" she asked, her voice full of curiosity.

"I don't know," Kurchi replied, her voice steady but filled with wonder. "But wherever it leads, we'll go together."

As they moved deeper into the passage, the light from the doorway behind them began to fade, leaving them to follow the soft glow from the walls. The air grew cooler, and the passage seemed to stretch on endlessly.

Ghurni, who had been leading the way, paused and turned to face her friends. "Did you hear that?"

Kurchi and Meghna stopped, straining their ears. At first, there was only silence. But then, the faintest sound reached them—like the flutter of pages turning.

“It’s coming from ahead,” Ghurni said, her voice filled with both curiosity and concern.

They moved forward, and the sound grew louder. Soon, they came to a small alcove where the passage opened into a larger chamber. The room was filled with shelves stacked high with ancient books, scrolls, and strange artifacts. The air smelled of dust and old paper, and the room hummed with the same quiet energy they had felt in the library earlier.

But something was different here.

Kurchi felt a shiver run down her spine. The room was still—too still—and her heart raced. The books, many of them old and worn, seemed to shift ever so slightly, like they were aware of their presence. It felt as if the room itself was alive, waiting for them to uncover its secrets.

“I don’t like this,” Meghna muttered, her voice nervous.

Ghurni moved forward, her brow furrowed as she examined one of the nearby shelves. “These books feel strange,” she said quietly. “They don’t seem real.”

Kurchi took a step forward, drawn to the center of the room. There, bathed in soft light, was a pedestal. On it lay a book unlike any they had seen before. It was bound in dark leather, and strange symbols were engraved on its surface, shifting and changing as Kurchi watched.

The girls exchanged uneasy glances.

“This book feels... different,” Kurchi whispered. “It’s calling to me.”

Ghurni frowned, her face full of caution. “Are you sure we should open it? It could be dangerous.”

But Meghna, her eyes wide with excitement, nodded eagerly. “We came this far, right? We have to keep going.”

Kurchi hesitated for a moment, her hand hovering over the book. But then, she reached out and touched it. The moment her fingers made contact, the symbols on the cover began to glow, casting an eerie, pale light across the room.

The girls stepped back instinctively, fear creeping into their hearts. But Kurchi’s hand remained on the book, as if something unseen was guiding her.

With a soft rustling sound, the book opened.

The air around them seemed to shift. A rush of wind filled the room, even though there was no source of air. The pages of the book flipped rapidly, too fast for anyone to read them. Kurchi, her heart pounding in her chest, watched in awe as the words on the pages shifted and changed, like the book was alive.

“Kurchi,” Ghurni whispered, her voice full of excitement, “what’s happening?”

Kurchi’s fingers trembled as she reached deeper into the book, feeling its energy pulse through her. “I think... it’s showing us something.”

Suddenly, the book stopped. The pages froze on one particular page. It was a map—a map that seemed to stretch on forever, covering vast landscapes, strange cities, and places they had never seen. But in the center of the map was the symbol they recognized—a glowing Heartstone.

"That's it," Meghna said, her voice shaking. "That's the Heartstone from the trials."

Kurchi nodded, feeling a chill crawl up her spine. "But how... how does this map know?"

Ghurni took a step closer, her eyes fixed on the map. "It's showing us a path," she said, her voice full of awe. "A path we need to follow."

The map shimmered, and a glowing line appeared, tracing a route from their current location to an unknown destination. As Kurchi stared at the glowing trail, a sense of purpose filled her.

"We need to follow this path," Kurchi said, her voice strong and confident. "It's our next step."

Ghurni and Meghna nodded, their faces filled with determination. Together, they turned away from the book. The map was now etched in their minds.

Chapter 19
The Path Ahead

The map glowed faintly in the dim light of the chamber, its intricate design pulling Kurchi in. She couldn't look away, feeling as if the path was meant for her—and for them. The weight of it settled heavily on her shoulders. The world beyond the hidden library was waiting, but Kurchi wasn't sure if they were ready. Her friends, however, were already looking toward the next step.

"We have to go," Ghurni said, breaking the silence, her voice calm yet filled with determination. She stepped closer to the map, her fingers tracing the glowing line. "This is the only way forward."

Kurchi hesitated for just a moment longer, her mind racing. The world they had uncovered seemed far bigger than they'd imagined. There were more trials to face, more challenges to overcome, and more mysteries to unravel. But they couldn't turn back now. Not when they were so close to understanding what the Heartstone truly was—and what it had to do with them.

"You're right," Kurchi said, finally breaking the silence. "We can't stop now."

Ghurni turned and walked toward the entrance, but before she left the room, she looked over her shoulder at Kurchi. "Are you okay?"

Kurchi's heart skipped a beat. Was she okay? How could she be? But she smiled softly and nodded. "I'm fine. Let's just figure this out together."

Together. That was the only way they had ever done anything—and it was the only way they would make it through this.

Meghna was already at the doorway, waiting for them. "Come on, let's go! Who knows what we'll find next?"

The girls exchanged a final glance, the weight of what lay ahead hanging in the air, but they stepped into the corridor together, their steps in sync as always. The passage seemed endless as it stretched before them, but Kurchi felt a strange pull—a sense that they were on the right path. The map, now glowing brightly in her mind, led them forward, each step seeming to match the rhythm of her heartbeat.

After what felt like hours, the passage opened into a wide, circular chamber, its walls lined with ancient inscriptions. At the far end stood another doorway, a single stone archway with symbols similar to those in the book, glowing faintly as if alive.

"We're getting closer," Kurchi murmured, her voice filled with awe.

Ghurni nodded, her gaze fixed on the doorway. "I think we need to go through that."

"Let's do it," Meghna said with a confident smile, and without another word, she marched forward, leading the way.

As they approached the archway, the symbols on the stone began to glow brighter, the faint hum of energy vibrating through the air. When they reached the door, it didn't open automatically, like the others they had encountered. Instead, there was a small indentation in the center of the arch—like a place meant to hold something.

The map. The Heartstone. Kurchi's mind raced as she connected the pieces.

"I think we need to place the Heartstone there," Kurchi said, her heart skipping a beat. "That's what will open this door."

The Heartstone fit perfectly into the indentation on the archway. Kurchi placed it carefully, and as she did, the symbols around the arch began to glow brighter and brighter. The stone around them hummed with energy, as if the very walls were alive.

A soft click sounded, and the stone archway slowly began to rise.

The door was opening.

But as the stone doors parted, the girls realized they weren't alone.

From the shadows at the far side of the chamber, a figure stepped forward. It was tall and cloaked, its features hidden in shadow. But there was no mistaking the aura of power that surrounded it. The air around the figure seemed to shimmer, and its presence seemed to distort the very fabric of reality.

Kurchi froze. "Who... who are you?"

The figure spoke in a voice like the rustling of dry leaves, soft and unsettling. "I am the Guardian of the Path. You are the chosen ones, but your journey is not over yet."

The figure took a step closer, its gaze fixing on each of them in turn.

"You have proven yourselves worthy," it continued, "but there is much more to learn, much more to uncover. The Heartstone is but one piece of a much larger puzzle. And you have only begun to understand its true power."

Kurchi, Ghurni, and Meghna exchanged uncertain glances. This was it. The moment they had been working toward, and yet, it felt like the beginning of something far greater than they could have imagined.

The Guardian's eyes glinted with an ancient wisdom, and it smiled, a small, knowing smile.

"Are you ready to step into the unknown?" the Guardian asked.

Kurchi's heart pounded in her chest. They had no choice. They had come this far, and they could never turn back.

"We're ready," she said, her voice steady and sure.

The Guardian's smile widened. "Then follow me."

Chapter 20
The Guardian 's Test

The air felt different here. More oppressive, yet charged with an odd sense of purpose. The Guardian's eyes gleamed as it stepped forward, its presence commanding attention. Its movements were fluid, almost like the wind, and as it spoke, the chamber seemed to shift, becoming more than just a place—it became a doorway to another world.

"Come," the Guardian beckoned, gesturing toward the now opened archway. The stone walls surrounding them seemed to breathe in time with the figure's voice, a steady pulse resonating deep within Kurchi's chest. "The true test begins now."

The girls exchanged uneasy glances. This was it. This was the moment they had been preparing for, but something about the Guardian made the air thicker, the uncertainty greater.

"Are you sure we're ready for this?" Meghna asked, her voice quieter than usual, but still filled with that indomitable curiosity that had always driven her.

Kurchi looked toward Ghurni, who met her gaze with a calm, almost peaceful look in her eyes. It was as though the logic of the riddles and puzzles they had faced so far had given her a strange sense of confidence—something that Kurchi envied. Yet, deep down, she knew they had no choice. They had already come too far.

"We have to go," Kurchi said, nodding toward the entrance. "This is what we were meant to do."

Ghurni gave a small nod, and Meghna, was already stepping forward, eyes wide with excitement. Without another word, the three of them followed the Guardian into the passage beyond the archway.

As they passed through the stone doorway, the temperature seemed to drop. The passage was unlike any they had encountered before. The walls were smooth and cold to the touch, covered in intricate carvings that appeared to shift with every step they took. There was an unnatural stillness in the air, but it didn't feel menacing. It felt... ancient. As though this place had been waiting for them for centuries.

After walking for what felt like an eternity, the passage opened into a vast, open chamber. The ceiling was high above them, lost in shadows, and the floor was covered in intricate patterns, almost like a labyrinth. In the center of the room was a large stone pedestal, much like the one where they had found the Heartstone, but this one was different. It had multiple levels and various indentations that seemed to shift as the girls approached.

The Guardian halted in front of the pedestal and turned to face them. "This is where your final test begins," it said, its voice echoing in the stillness. "To truly prove yourselves worthy of the Heartstone, you must solve the trials that await you here. Only then will you be granted access to the Heartstone's full power."

Kurchi felt her breath catch in her throat. They had solved riddles, they had unlocked secrets, but this... this felt different. She had no idea what to expect next.

"What kind of trials?" Ghurni asked, her voice steady but with an edge of curiosity.

The Guardian smiled faintly, as though it knew something they didn't. "You will each face a trial tailored to your strengths and weaknesses. Only by overcoming them will you unlock the next step of your journey."

Meghna shifted nervously, her hands fiddling with the edge of her sleeve. "And what happens if we fail?"

The Guardian's gaze softened slightly, but there was still a sense of gravity in its eyes. "Failure does not mean defeat, but it will delay your progress. You must face your fears, your weaknesses, and your doubts. Only by confronting them will you be ready for what lies ahead."

Kurchi took a deep breath, glancing at her friends. They had always faced things together—this would be no different. But she felt a sense of uncertainty stir inside her. What were they about to face?

The Guardian raised one hand, and the pedestal seemed to shift, the carvings on the walls flickering like flame. "You must each step forward and face the trial of your heart. This is your moment of reckoning."

Before any of them could respond, the ground beneath them rumbled, and suddenly, Kurchi found herself standing alone in the center of the chamber, separated from Ghurni and Meghna by an invisible barrier.

A deep voice boomed through the room, and the pedestal in front of Kurchi began to spin slowly. "Kurchi, your trial is to face the fear you carry within your voice."

Kurchi's heart skipped a beat. Fear? But her voice was her gift. How could it be the source of her fear? She had always been proud of it, of what it could do.

But as the pedestal continued to spin, the voice grew louder, echoing through the room. "Your gift, your power, is a double-edged sword. It can heal, it can protect, but it can also hurt. You must confront the shadow of doubt that lies within you."

The room around her started to distort. Her breath quickened, and suddenly, she found herself standing in a dark, empty space. The walls closed in around her, and she could feel the weight of the silence pressing in on her chest. It was like the absence of sound was suffocating her.

And then, she heard it. The whispers.

What if you fail? What if they don't believe in you? What if your voice causes harm instead of good?

Kurchi's knees trembled. She had never heard her doubts so loudly, so vividly. She had always been certain of her powers—her ability to sing, to reach others with her voice. But now, all of a sudden, it felt like a burden. What if she was wrong? What if her voice wasn't the gift she thought it was, but something that could destroy?

Tears stung her eyes, but she blinked them away. No, she thought fiercely. I can't let this stop me.

Kurchi closed her eyes, taking a deep breath. She could feel her voice, deep within her chest, alive and waiting. It wasn't the source of her fear—it was her strength.

The whispers began to fade as Kurchi opened her mouth, a soft, gentle note escaping her lips. It wasn't a song—it was just a sound, a simple note. But as the sound reverberated through the space, the walls around her began to crumble away.

She didn't need to prove anything to anyone. She didn't need to be perfect. All she had to do was trust herself.

Her voice grew stronger, filling the space with its melody. The chamber transformed around her, the dark walls dissolving into light. The fear that had threatened to swallow her was replaced by a quiet confidence.

Kurchi's voice wasn't just a gift. It was a part of her—something she could control, something she could trust. And she wasn't going to let fear take that away.

The space around her cleared, and Kurchi was back in the chamber with her friends. The invisible barrier had vanished, and the Guardian was standing before them once more.

"You have passed the first trial," it said, its voice calm. "Now, your friends will face their own trials."

Kurchi turned to Ghurni and Meghna, her heart swelling with pride. They had faced their fears before, but this was different. This trial was more than just a puzzle—it was about confronting the very essence of who they were.

She couldn't wait to see how they would rise to the challenge.

Chapter 21
The Riddle of Time

The air felt thick with anticipation as Kurchi, Ghurni, and Meghna stood in the center of the grand chamber, the walls echoing with the whispers of the trials they had just faced. Kurchi's heart was still racing, the memory of her confrontation with her fears lingering at the edges of her mind. She had passed her trial. But the trials weren't over yet. Now, it was Ghurni and Meghna's turn.

The Guardian's presence loomed over them, its form flickering like a mirage in the dim light of the chamber. It didn't speak for a moment, as though allowing the girls to catch their breath, to absorb the gravity of the moment. Kurchi exchanged a glance with Ghurni. The calm, determined look in her friend's eyes told her that Ghurni was ready.

Meghna, on the other hand, was shifting from foot to foot, her usual energy replaced by an almost nervous restlessness. But Kurchi knew Meghna well enough to understand that the fear of the unknown was something she could overcome. When it came down to it, Meghna was as brave as they came.

"Your trial is next," the Guardian finally spoke, its voice deep and steady, reverberating in the silence. "Ghurni, you must face the Riddle of Time."

Ghurni's brows furrowed in concentration. "The Riddle of Time?"

The Guardian nodded, its glowing eyes flickering. "The riddle you will face is not just one of words, but one of perception. Time is a fragile thing—it bends, it stretches, it can even break. To solve this riddle, you must see beyond the surface, into the very essence of time itself."

Ghurni took a deep breath. As a riddle solver, she was used to puzzles and mysteries, but this… this sounded different. It wasn't just a riddle to be solved; it was an experience, an exploration of something far more abstract.

"I'm ready," Ghurni said, her voice steady.

The Guardian extended a hand, and a swirling vortex of light appeared before them. It shifted, forming into an intricate clock face, its hands spinning rapidly in reverse, then forward again. The numbers on the clock were distorted, blurry as if they were constantly changing.

"The riddle begins now," the Guardian intoned. "Solve it, and you will pass the trial. Fail, and time will remain lost to you."

Before Ghurni could respond, a voice echoed from the clock itself, its words like a chorus of whispers blending together.

"I have no body, but I am a part of every living thing. I move with no sound, yet I am ever present. I can bend, I can break, and I can heal. What am I?"

The riddle lingered in the air, vibrating with the pulse of time itself. Ghurni stepped forward, her mind already working through the layers of the puzzle. Time. Time itself was the answer, wasn't it?

But was that too simple? Was there something more to it?

Ghurni closed her eyes and listened. The riddle was more than just a question. It was a key, a guide to understanding the very essence of time. She felt a pull in her chest, like a faint rhythm, an unspoken answer tugging at the edges of her mind.

The clock in front of her continued to spin, its hands moving faster, its numbers shifting. With each turn, the riddle seemed to change, slipping further away, just out of reach. She had to focus.

Ghurni opened her eyes again, her gaze fixed on the spinning clock. The answer was there. She could feel it.

"I think I know," she murmured aloud.

Kurchi and Meghna exchanged a quick glance, but neither spoke. They both knew this was Ghurni's trial. They could only watch and wait.

Ghurni stepped forward, closing the distance between herself and the swirling clock. The riddle was clearer now.

"I am time itself," she said, her voice ringing with confidence. "I move in cycles, I am always in motion, yet I am invisible. You cannot touch me, but you can feel my passing. I am the one thing that is constant, no matter what changes around me. And without me, nothing exists."

The clock's hands suddenly froze, and the numbers on its face became sharp and clear. The swirling vortex of light calmed, its spinning slowing to a stop.

Ghurni stood still for a moment, feeling the weight of the riddle's resolution settle in her chest. She had done it. She had solved the Riddle of Time.

The Guardian nodded, its approval evident in its expressionless face. "Well done, Ghurni. You have proven yourself worthy. The trial is complete."

The clock disappeared, and the room returned to its previous stillness. Ghurni turned to Kurchi and Meghna, a smile tugging at the corners of her lips. The sense of relief was palpable. She had passed.

Meghna, who had been fidgeting nervously, was the first to rush forward, throwing her arms around Ghurni in an enthusiastic hug. “I knew you could do it!” Meghna exclaimed, her voice full of excitement.

Kurchi grinned, her heart swelling with pride. Ghurni had done it—she had faced the trial, and not only solved it, but understood the deeper meaning behind it. The Riddle of Time had been no easy feat, but Ghurni had approached it with the calm determination that they all admired so much.

But before they could celebrate, the Guardian spoke again, its tone turning serious.

“Now, it is Meghna’s turn. You must face your trial, Meghna.”

The energy in the room shifted as the Guardian turned toward the youngest of the three friends. Meghna’s grin faded slightly, her playful energy replaced by a more introspective look. She stepped forward, her shoulders squared, but Kurchi could see the nerves flickering in her eyes.

“Meghna,” the Guardian continued, “Your trial is one of memory and perception. You must face the Test of Reflection.”

Meghna tilted her head in confusion. “The Test of Reflection?”

The Guardian nodded. “In this trial, Meghna, you will face a series of memories—some your own, some not. You must discern the truth from illusion, for not all memories are as they seem.”

Meghna took a deep breath, her usual bravado returning. She had always been good at remembering things, and she trusted her memory above all else. This test would be a challenge, but it wasn’t impossible. She had her friends by her side, and they had faced their trials together.

“I’m ready,” Meghna said, her voice firm.

The Guardian stepped aside, revealing a shimmering, mirrored surface that stretched from the floor to the ceiling. The surface rippled like water, and Meghna could see faint images reflected within it. A series of snapshots—memories—flashed before her eyes.

The first image was of her at her old home, her mother smiling as she handed her a small book. The book seemed important, but Meghna didn’t recognize it. The second image showed her walking through a forest, a sense of familiarity washing over her, though she had never been there. Each image was accompanied by a soft voice calling her name, but the words were distorted, as though the memories were being filtered through a fog.

"What's happening?" Meghna whispered, her brow furrowing as she stared into the reflections.

The Guardian's voice answered, "The memories you are seeing may not be your own. It is up to you to recognize which are true and which are false. Your task is to discern the truth hidden within the illusions."

Meghna’s heart began to race. She had always relied on her memory, her ability to remember the tiniest details, to connect the dots in ways others couldn't. But now, she was faced with the possibility that some of her memories might not be real.

The first memory shifted again, and Meghna felt her stomach churn as she saw a reflection of herself standing at the edge of a cliff, looking out over an endless, dark ocean. She had never been to a cliff like that, never stood over an abyss that stretched into nothingness.

Suddenly, the reflection of herself smiled—a smile that wasn’t her own. It was cold, unsettling.

"You're not real," Meghna murmured to herself. "This isn’t real."

The reflection seemed to mock her, its smile stretching wider as the voice of the Guardian echoed in the distance. "You must trust your instincts, Meghna. The illusion is not what it seems."

Meghna closed her eyes for a moment, taking in a deep breath. Her mind raced, her memories flashing before her. She had always known the truth about herself, the things she could remember. The images before her now, the false reflections—they were lies. She could feel it deep inside her.

When she opened her eyes, she focused on the mirror once more. She stared into the reflection, this time seeing only herself—no dark cliffs, no mocking smiles. Just Meghna, standing firm, unwavering.

"I remember," she whispered to herself. "I know who I am."

And with that, the mirror shimmered and dissolved into nothingness.

Chapter 22
The Path of Unity

The mirror faded into nothingness, leaving only a warm glow where it had stood. Meghna remained still for a moment, her chest rising and falling in slow, steady breaths. She had passed the Test of Reflection. The trial had tried to twist her sense of memory and identity, but she had held strong. When she turned back to Kurchi and Ghurni, they were already rushing toward her. Ghurni wrapped her in a tight hug first, and then Kurchi joined them both, arms encircling her two best friends in a moment of relief and triumph.

"You did it," Kurchi said softly. "You saw through it all."

"I almost didn't," Meghna whispered. "It was… weird. Like my memories were tangled with someone else's. But in the end, I knew who I was."

"I knew you would," Ghurni said with a proud grin. "Your memory is sharper than a porcupine's quill!"

Kurchi laughed, her eyes bright. "I don't know if that's a real saying, but it should be."

They stood together, arms linked, while the chamber around them shimmered once more. The Guardian had not moved during Meghna's trial, and now it stepped forward, its translucent form pulsing with a soft blue light.

"You have each faced your individual trials," it said, its voice echoing with a gentle reverence. "You have shown courage, wisdom, and strength of heart. But the Temple is not yet done with you."

The chamber darkened. A hum vibrated in the stone beneath their feet.

“There is one final path you must walk,” the Guardian continued. “A path that no one walks alone. This is the Path of Unity.”

Suddenly, a great door carved with ancient symbols began to open at the far end of the chamber. A warm golden light spilled through the crack, growing brighter as the door slowly widened. The hum intensified, not threatening but full of energy—alive with purpose. Kurchi, Ghurni, and Meghna instinctively reached for each other’s hands.

“Together?” Meghna asked.

The moment their fingers intertwined, Kurchi felt a familiar whisper stir deep inside her — ancient, steady, certain.

"One who sings the stones awake.

One who sees the riddles within shadows.

One who guards the ember of memory."

The old prophecy — it was no longer a riddle, no longer a mystery.

It was *them.*

They weren’t just walking the path together.

They *were* the Path of Unity.

The golden light grew stronger, wrapping them in a soft, living glow.

Without hesitation, they stepped forward through the ancient doorway — toward whatever waited beyond.

Inside, the golden light faded as the girls crossed into the next room. They found themselves in a wide, circular space with high, domed ceilings. The walls were covered in murals—vibrant and old, showing children like them standing before great temples, holding glowing objects, facing shadowy creatures, and unlocking hidden doors.

"It's like… this place remembers all the ones who came before us," Ghurni whispered, her eyes scanning the paintings.

In the center of the room stood a low pedestal with three indents carved into it: a treble clef, an eye, a flame — symbols of the girls' powers. The pedestal was surrounded by three stone platforms, each etched with a puzzle or challenge. The Guardian's voice echoed once more, but it came not from behind them, but from within the walls themselves.

"This is your final trial in the Temple of the Forgotten. Here, you must act not as individuals—but as one. You must solve the puzzles not by separating your gifts, but by combining them."

Kurchi stepped toward the pedestal. "This is what the library and the map were leading us to. Not just us learning our powers—but learning each other."

Ghurni nodded, stepping onto the platform with the eye symbol. "Then let's start. Together."

The first puzzle began as Ghurni stepped onto the platform. Immediately, the walls shimmered, and part of the chamber morphed into a room filled with floating orbs. Each orb emitted a soft sound—some musical notes, others whispers of riddles. Kurchi walked up beside her. “This is for both of us, I think.” A message appeared in glowing letters above them: “When the tune and the meaning become one, the path shall be revealed.”

Ghurni’s eyes lit up. “It’s a sound-and-riddle match. We have to combine the right musical note with the right riddle.”

Meghna watched from the side, fascinated. “Kurchi, sing something.”

Kurchi nodded and began to hum gently. As she sang, some of the orbs glowed brighter, while others dimmed.

“There! That one,” Ghurni pointed. “That orb brightened when you hit the C note. And the riddle it whispered was—‘I fly without wings, I cry without eyes.’ That’s ‘cloud.’”

Kurchi sang again, shifting the tone. Another orb flared. “That one’s G sharp,” she said, “and the riddle was about something that travels but has no feet…”

“Wind!” Ghurni answered immediately.

They continued, matching sound and meaning, voice and riddle. As each match was made, the orb drifted downward and dissolved. When all the right combinations had been made, the chamber shimmered again—and the next platform rose.

Now it was Meghna’s turn. She stepped onto her platform, and immediately the world around them blurred. When their vision cleared, the girls found themselves inside a large maze—walls of stone, shifting paths, and flickering torches.

“There are clues hidden in the maze,” said Meghna. “But not all of them are correct. I have to remember which ones we’ve seen before in the temple and which ones are false leads.”

Ghurni frowned. “But how will we help you?”

“You already did,” Meghna replied. “You were with me through every part of the journey. I’ll need both of you to guide me. Use your voice, Kurchi—use direction. And Ghurni, your riddles—they might be the key to interpreting the signs.”

As they walked through the maze, the walls began to whisper riddles and songs. Some paths repeated memories from earlier—like the Guardian’s riddle or the hallway of floating books. Others were twisted, false paths meant to confuse them.

But with Meghna’s sharp memory, Kurchi’s voice guiding their steps, and Ghurni’s logic solving the puzzle signs, they navigated the maze in record time. When they reached the center, a final torch flared with golden fire. A hidden door opened, revealing the third and final platform.

In the last part of the chamber stood a stone pedestal with a shimmering orb floating above it—the Heartstone. The artifact that the Guardian had spoken of. It pulsed faintly, locked behind magical glyphs and runes. All three girls stepped forward at once.

"This is it," Kurchi said. "The object we were meant to find."

Ghurni looked at the glyphs, her eyes narrowing. "They're layered like riddles, but with shifting patterns."

"And it's responding to our presence," Meghna added, pointing to the glow that increased with every step they took.

A small inscription appeared: "Only hearts that beat as one may unlock the power of the Heartstone."

"Like a harmony," Kurchi said. "We need to do this… together."

Meghna placed her hand on the stone. "I'll follow your lead."

Ghurni did the same. "And I'll decipher as we go."

Kurchi closed her eyes and began to sing—not loud, but soft and true. It was the lullaby her mother once sang to her, the same song that had awakened the magical book weeks ago. As the notes floated through the air, the glyphs began to pulse.

Ghurni spoke softly between the verses, solving the riddles aloud: "What walks on four legs in the morning…"

"Man," whispered Meghna. "I remember that."

With each line sung, each answer spoken, the lock around the Heartstone broke away, glowing brighter and brighter—until with a final hum, the orb rose into the air. It hovered above their heads and then split into three beams of light, each touching a pendant they didn't remember wearing—but now shimmered on their necks.

"The Heartstone has chosen," the Guardian's voice came again. "And so, the protectors are formed anew."

Chapter 23
The Secret Beneath the Flame

The golden glow from the Heartstone slowly faded into a soft warmth inside their pendants. Each pendant was different—Kurchi's shimmered like a drop of morning dew with a treble clef inscribed on it. Ghurni's had a tiny glowing eye, ever watchful, etched in delicate patterns. Meghna's sparkled with a flame —a symbol of memory and time. None of them spoke for a long moment. The entire Temple seemed to sigh around them, as though the place itself had been waiting for this—waiting for them. The chamber became still, lit only by a few lingering wisps of light where the Heartstone had hovered. Then the Guardian's voice returned, calm and steady.

"The Heartstone has accepted you. You are now its guardians. But its power is not yet complete. One final path remains—the place where the stone was forged, hidden beneath the Eternal Flame."

Meghna tilted her head. "The Eternal Flame?"

Kurchi took a slow breath. "There was a flame on one of the old temple murals. It burned in the center of a circle, beneath the earth."

Ghurni snapped her fingers. "Yes! And there were stairs carved below it. Like a hidden chamber. Maybe that's where the Heartstone is meant to be anchored."

The floor beneath them trembled faintly—then, without warning, a ring of fire burst to life in the center of the chamber. Not a roaring fire, but a quiet one—strangely controlled, dancing in a perfect circle on stone that should never burn. In the center of the flames was a spiral staircase, leading downward.

Kurchi blinked. “Well, that’s new.”

“Looks like the final trial begins below,” Ghurni said, adjusting her glasses.

“Let’s go,” Meghna said simply. “We’re ready.”

And together, they stepped into the flame. The staircase was carved from old stone, cool beneath their feet. The air grew colder as they descended, though the circle of fire above them remained lit—casting a glow that slowly faded with each step. Their path spiraled down, down, until they reached a wide tunnel, lined with glowing blue runes. At the end stood a door. It looked ancient—far older than the temple itself—covered in carvings of mythical creatures: winged horses, giant serpents, tree spirits, and children holding lights in their hands. Meghna stepped forward and brushed the surface of the door. Immediately, the carvings began to move—animated by some unseen magic. The creatures slithered, flew, and shimmered, forming a kind of story: Three girls standing before a mountain. A library with glowing books. A hidden temple. A stone pulsing with light. And finally, a great darkness looming behind them—shapeless, silent, vast.

“What is that?” Kurchi whispered. “That shadow at the end…”

“I think it’s the threat the Guardian warned us about,” Ghurni said quietly. “Something that was once sealed away—something only the Heartstone could keep in check.”

Meghna nodded. "And now… it's waking up." The door opened with a slow groan, revealing a massive underground dome. In the center of the space burned the Eternal Flame—not on wood or fuel, but floating mid-air, suspended above a stone altar. The fire glowed with hues of red, orange, and gold—but occasionally, it shimmered with blue or green, as though responding to something unseen. The altar beneath it had three shallow indents. Each one pulsed faintly, shaped like the pendants now hanging around their necks.

"The final step," Ghurni said, walking forward with awe. "We return what we've been given."

"No," Kurchi corrected. "We share it. We don't lose our powers. We just… connect them to the Heartstone."

They stepped forward in silence and placed their pendants into the grooves. As soon as the last one clicked into place, the flame above erupted—not wildly, but with purpose. A spiral of golden fire shot upward, twisting around the chamber, lighting every rune on the walls. The air hummed. The temple trembled. The walls whispered.

Then a voice—not the Guardian's, but a memory—filled the room.

"To those who are chosen: hold fast to the light. The darkness that sleeps shall stir again. But the fire remembers. And now, so shall you."

The flame descended, not burning, but wrapping them in warmth. Each girl felt it differently—Kurchi heard it as a song, Ghurni saw it as dancing equations and riddles, and

Meghna felt it as a thousand memories blooming behind her eyes. And then, just as suddenly, it ended.

The pendants reappeared around their necks, warmer than before. But they were no longer just tokens—they were keys. Anchors to the Heartstone's power. The altar cracked open slightly, and a new object rose from within: a golden compass, glowing softly.

Meghna picked it up. "Another artifact?"

Ghurni examined the markings. "No... this is more than a map. I think this compass points not north, but to places of magic—places like this one."

Kurchi smiled. "Then maybe our adventure isn't over yet."

A pulse of energy rolled through the chamber, and suddenly the walls began to shift. The murals melted away. The chamber folded in on itself like a closing book.

"We need to get out," Ghurni said quickly.

"But where—" Kurchi began, before a circle of light opened before them. A portal. Familiar. Friendly.

"Home," Meghna said with a grin. "Finally."

They emerged in Kurchi's rooftop room, the evening breeze brushing their faces like nothing had happened. The dusty bookshelves were still there. The snacks left behind had gone cold. A distant honk from the street below brought them back to the present. It had only been a few hours since they left. Kurchi's father poked his head into the room, carrying a tray of warm samosas and lemonade. "Girls! I thought you'd gone quiet. All okay?"

The three of them blinked, glanced at one another, and then nodded—just a little too fast.

"Just reading," Kurchi said quickly.

Her father raised an eyebrow. "Reading must be really exciting these days."

He smiled, set the tray down, and turned to leave—but his eyes paused on the corner of the room. On the shelf where the magical book had first appeared. He stared at it for a second too long. Then turned back to them.

"Where did you say you found that book again?" he asked casually.

The girls froze.

"It was just… lying around," Meghna said quickly.

"Hmm." Kurchi's father looked thoughtful. "Strange. That book used to belong to a very old friend of mine."

The girls stared at him.

"But that's a story for another day," he added with a wink. "Eat while it's hot."

And with that, he left, humming softly to himself.

Kurchi, Ghurni, and Meghna sat in silence for a moment. The flame of the Eternal Fire still flickered inside them. The pendants around their necks pulsed gently. The golden compass glowed faintly on the table between them.

Chapter 24
The Keeper of Flames

That night, Kurchi couldn't sleep. The stars were shining brighter than usual, almost as if they were whispering something to her. She quietly wrapped a thin cotton sheet around her shoulders and went up to the rooftop. The town below was peaceful, but the book on her desk was glowing softly.

She opened it.

More writing had appeared, written in a swirling, flame-like script:

When flame forgets its light,

Seek the Keeper deep in the night.

Beyond the pond where moonflowers bloom,

Lies a temple of fire, an ancient tomb.

Kurchi’s heart skipped a beat. A temple of fire. The second temple!

The next morning, after a quick meeting on the rooftop the girls set off toward the east. The compass led them through neighborhoods, across fields, and finally to a small, quiet pond called Moonflower Pond. The water shimmered in the sunlight, and the white flowers around the edge only bloomed at night. It was a peaceful place, but Kurchi felt something special about it.

“There’s no temple,” Ghurni said, looking around.

“Maybe it’s not visible yet,” Kurchi said. “The poem mentioned something about deep night.”

Meghna frowned. "Do we wait until it gets dark?"

“Or maybe until the moonlight hits the right spot,” Ghurni guessed.

The girls sat down and waited, their eyes watching the pond. As the sky grew darker, the first moonbeam touched the water, and something began to happen. The moonflowers turned, as if they were watching the girls. Then, with a soft ripple, stone steps rose from beneath the water, leading down into the earth.

The steps led them into a hidden cavern beneath the pond. The walls were made of dark stone, glowing with lines of orange, like cracks filled with glowing embers. Torches lit themselves as they walked deeper into the cave. At the center of the room was a platform surrounded by floating orbs of fire. In the middle sat a tall figure, cloaked in red and gold. His hair was the color of fire, and his eyes burned softly, like lanterns in the dark.

“I am the Keeper of Flames,” the figure said, his voice rumbling like the sound of coals crackling.

Kurchi stepped forward, her heart racing. "We’ve come to find the second Heartstone."

The Keeper studied her carefully. “And have you passed the first trial?”

“Yes,” Ghurni replied. “At the Temple of the shifting wind.”

“Then you must prove yourselves worthy of the flame,” the Keeper said, raising his hand. The fire orbs swirled around them, lighting up the cavern even brighter.

"The first test is for Meghna," the Keeper said, pointing to her. "The Flame of Memory."

Suddenly, a path of fire appeared in front of Meghna, lined with glowing images from her past—moments of fear, mistakes, and regret.

"Walk the path," the Keeper said. "Face what you fear to forget."

Meghna hesitated, but then, with a deep breath, she stepped forward. Each step showed a new memory—times when she had lost in a quiz, forgotten her friend's birthday, or hidden in fear when someone needed help. But Meghna kept walking.

At the end of the path, she stood before a mirror. In the reflection, she saw herself—not perfect, but strong and brave. The fire dimmed, and the Keeper nodded.

Next, it was Ghurni's turn.

"The Flame of Wisdom," the Keeper said. A riddle appeared in the air:

I do not speak, yet all hear me.

I cannot be seen, yet I carry light.

What am I?

Ghurni thought for a moment. "Sound? No… Wind? Maybe…" She glanced at Kurchi, then back at the Keeper. Then, softly, she said, "A song."

The flames flared brightly and then settled. "Correct," the Keeper said, smiling.

Now it was Kurchi's turn. The Keeper looked deep into her eyes. "The Flame of Voice. Sing not for magic, but for truth."

Kurchi took a deep breath, closed her eyes, and sang. Not the lullaby she usually sang, but a new song—a song about friendship, about courage, and about the power of finding light in the darkest places. As she sang, the flames danced, swirling around her.

The pedestal in front of them cracked open, and inside, glowing softly, was a crimson jewel shaped like a flame. The second Heartstone.

As Kurchi reached for it, the Keeper's expression changed. "Hurry," he said. "The third temple lies where stars once fell—but darkness rises faster now."

Ghurni frowned. "Do you mean the third guardian?"

"No," the Keeper replied. "The third Heartstone is in danger. The shadows are awake."

The walls around them began to shake. Outside, the moonflowers closed, and a cloud of crows circled above.

The Keeper placed a hand on Kurchi's shoulder. "Remember this: fire cannot fight alone. Light needs roots. Flame needs memory."

The temple began to darken, and the entrance behind them started to close. With the Heartstone in hand, the girls quickly raced back into the night. The real battle was just beginning. But now—they were ready.

Chapter 25
The Sky of Crows

The wind had changed.

Even as the girls climbed out of the hidden passage beneath Moonflower Pond, the air felt different—heavier, almost as if it was holding its breath. The trees were still. The night crickets had stopped their chirping, and a deep silence hung over everything. Above, the sky was filled with a black spiral of crows—hundreds, maybe even thousands—circling against the starry backdrop.

“Why are they flying like that?” Meghna whispered, holding the crimson Heartstone close to her chest, its warmth pulsing in her hands.

“They’re not flying,” Ghurni said slowly, scanning the dark shapes overhead. “They’re watching.”

The girls froze at the edge of the pond, the firelight of the Heartstone casting eerie, flickering shadows on their faces. The moon, once full and bright, was now hidden behind clouds, casting a thin, silvery veil over the land.

Kurchi could feel the Heartstone's pulse in her palm, steady but strong, as if it, too, was aware of the danger above them.

“They weren’t there before,” Kurchi said, her voice tight with unease. “It’s like they were waiting.”

“For us,” Meghna finished grimly.

Without another word, the girls sprang into action, their feet pounding against the dirt path as they sprinted through the night. Behind them, the crows’ caws echoed like sharp, broken laughter, filling the air with an eerie sense of dread.

Kurchi held the compass out as they ran, but the needle spun wildly, no longer pointing in any direction.

“It’s not working!” she cried, frustration creeping into her voice.

“Then we head home,” Ghurni said, her words coming quickly between breaths. “To the rooftop.”

Home. Safe. Together.

But the shadows had other plans.

Halfway through the trail, a wave of black feathers descended from above, forcing the girls to duck beneath a cluster of trees. The crows didn’t attack directly, but they surrounded them, circling closer and closer, blocking out the starlight. The air grew cold, and the oppressive feeling of being watched weighed heavily on them.

“Why aren’t they attacking?” Meghna gasped, panting.

“They’re herding us,” Ghurni realized, her sharp eyes catching the movement of the crows. “They’re trying to push us somewhere.”

Kurchi turned sharply, scanning the trees. “Then we run where they don’t want us to go.”

With the crows still circling, the girls veered off the main trail, heading toward the old stone bridge near the edge of the mango orchards. The bridge hadn’t been used in years. Its center was cracked, and one side was half crumbled, but it spanned a deep ditch and offered cover on the other side.

As soon as their feet hit the cold stone, the air grew even colder, and a single crow—larger than the others—landed in the center of the bridge, blocking their way. It stared at them with glowing red eyes, its feathers glistening like embers in the fading light.

Kurchi stepped forward, holding the Heartstone slightly raised in her palm. The crow didn't move, but a strange voice, raspy and distant, echoed in the air around them.

"Little voices and little flames,

You walk where fire dared not burn.

The third heart beats in hollow stone—

But the bookkeeper comes to turn."

Ghurni shivered, glancing around nervously. "What was that?"

"Not the crow," Kurchi whispered, eyes wide. "Something is speaking through it."

The crow tilted its head, then, as suddenly as it had appeared, it took flight, disappearing into the night. The rest of the flock scattered into the sky, their ominous presence breaking apart like a fading storm.

The spell, whatever it had been, was gone.

When they reached Kurchi's house, the lights were still on. Her father stood in the doorway, a worried expression on his face. "You're late. Too late."

"We're okay," Kurchi said quickly, holding up the glowing Heartstone. "We… found something."

Her father's gaze shifted from their faces to the glowing stone in Kurchi's hand, his concern deepening into something else—a kind of recognition.

"Come inside," he said softly, stepping aside to let them in.

They followed him upstairs to the rooftop room, the familiar smell of books, lemon tea, and toasted nuts wrapping around them like a comforting hug. As the door shut behind them, Kurchi's father set down a tray of snacks and motioned for them to sit.

Without asking, he looked at them seriously. "The Heartstones are waking again, aren't they?"

All three girls froze, their hearts skipping a beat.

"How do you know that?" Meghna asked, her voice barely a whisper.

Her father didn't answer right away. Instead, he leaned back in his chair, folding his hands together thoughtfully.

"When I was your age," he began, his voice quieter, "I used to dream of hidden libraries buried under hills, and riddles hidden in river stones. I used to think the stories my grandfather told me were just fairy tales."

He turned to Kurchi, his eyes soft but knowing. "But I kept listening. I kept reading. I collected what I could… waiting."

"For what?" Kurchi whispered, her voice trembling.

Her father smiled faintly, though it was a smile tinged with both sadness and hope. "For you. For children who would carry the book again."

He pointed to the glowing tome resting on the table. "That's not just a guide. It's a gate."

Ghurni opened the book, and this time, new writing appeared, inked in curling silver, like flames dancing across the page:

"Three hearts to guard the flame,

Three keys to seal the name.

Where star met earth, and glass was born,

The final truth shall be sworn."

"Where star met earth?" Meghna muttered, reading aloud. "What does that mean?"

"Starfall," Kurchi's father said suddenly. "There's an old legend about a meteorite that struck the eastern highlands centuries ago. The villagers still call it 'The Star Grave.'"

Kurchi's heart raced. "Then that's where we go next."

Her father's expression darkened, but he nodded. "But it's not just a journey anymore. The shadows know we're looking for the stones. They're following us."

Kurchi's father stood, his face set with determination. "Then it's time I do more than make snacks."

He pulled a large, dust-covered book from the top shelf. Its title read: Guardians of the Forgotten Flame.

He opened it to a page with a faded map. "This," he said, tracing a finger over the inked lines, "is where your final test begins."

Later that night, the girls stood on the rooftop, wrapped in shawls. The stars blinked above them, but there was something else, too—faint, shifting shadows in the corners of the sky. Crows, silent now, circled in the distance, moving in patterns that didn't quite make sense.

Meghna held the second Heartstone in her hand. Ghurni gripped the compass, which seemed to hum with restless energy. Kurchi held the book, its pages now filled with more secrets than ever before.

And in her mind, she heard something—a distant hum, like a song only she could hear.

The melody of the stones.

The harmony of the guardians.

"We're not just explorers anymore," Kurchi said, her voice full of quiet resolve.

Ghurni nodded. "We're protectors."

"Then let's protect it together," Meghna added.

And far off in the east, a faint red glow pulsed across the horizon, a sign of the challenges yet to come.

Chapter 26
The Star Grave

The sun rose over the eastern horizon, casting golden light over the fields and rooftops of their town, but the girls were already awake. Kurchi's rooftop room was cluttered with open books, old scrolls, and half-eaten snacks. A quiet tension hummed in the air. They all knew what came next.

Kurchi's father, still in his worn cotton kurta, stood by the table with a hand-drawn map laid out before him. His voice was steady but low. "The Star Grave lies beyond the outer mango groves, near the edge of the Rajabari Forest. It's an ancient impact site. Locals say nothing grows there, not even weeds."

Ghurni traced the lines of the map with her finger. "There's no path leading there."

"That's because it was erased from maps long ago," he said, eyes thoughtful. "It wasn't meant to be found again."

Kurchi exchanged a glance with her friends. "But we're going to find it."

The girls packed quickly: water bottles, flashlights, rope, a few snacks, a compass that now flickered with blue sparks, and the magical book, now heavier than ever. The Heartstone pulsed inside Kurchi's satchel like a heartbeat, warm and urgent. Meghna tied her shoelaces tighter. "We might be walking straight into another trap."

"Then let's walk smart," Ghurni replied, pocketing a notebook filled with her own riddle notes.

Kurchi's father handed her a small wooden box. Inside was a strange pendant: silver with a symbol shaped like a starburst.

"This belonged to my grandfather," he said. "He claimed it was forged from the fallen star itself. It may help you recognize the true heart of the grave."

Kurchi nodded, grateful but curious. "Did he ever go there?"

"He tried," her father said quietly. "But he never came back."

The journey took them past the mango orchards, across a rickety bamboo bridge, and into the edge of the Rajabari Forest. Sunlight trickled through the tall trees, but the deeper they went, the quieter it became. No birds. No rustling. Even the wind seemed to hold its breath.

The compass trembled in Meghna's hand, the needle jerking now and then as if confused. "I don't think it wants to go this way," she murmured.

But they pressed on, following faint carvings in the trees—ancient symbols that matched the pendant's starburst.

Finally, they emerged into a clearing. It was unlike anything they had ever seen.

The clearing was massive—an almost perfect circle of barren land surrounded by twisted trees. The ground was charred black, as if burned centuries ago, and in the center was a deep crater, filled with jagged rocks, broken shards of glassy stone, and a strange humming vibration in the air.

At the edge of the crater stood three tall pillars, each carved with a familiar symbol: a treble clef for Kurchi, an eye for Ghurni, and a flame for Meghna.

"The final temple," Kurchi whispered. "It's not underground or hidden in a pond. It's… fallen from the sky."

Ghurni stepped forward and touched one of the pillars. A sudden glow pulsed from its center. The pillar shimmered, and a symbol appeared—another riddle.

"Speak the name that has no sound.

Hear the voice that cannot speak.

Seek the flame that holds no heat.

Then only will you find what you seek."

"What does that even mean?" Meghna asked, scanning the riddle.

Kurchi stared into the crater. The stones within shimmered faintly, as if hiding something just below the surface. "I think this temple isn't made of bricks," she said. "It's made of riddles, illusions… and memory."

When Kurchi stood before her pillar and sang a soft tune—her childhood lullaby—the ground beneath her lit up in blue. But this time, the melody echoed back at her in a distorted tone, as if the place was listening. Then the earth shook.

From the crater rose a shape—a floating mirror of mist. In it, Kurchi saw herself—but silent. Her mouth moved, but no sound came out.

"I… can't sing," Kurchi gasped. "Not in the vision. Not in the test."

"It's the trial," her father's words echoed in her memory. "Each Heartstone must be earned, not taken."

Kurchi had to reach into her own fear—not just of losing her power, but of never having had it at all. She breathed in, steadied herself, and began to hum without sound, letting her emotion carry the melody in her mind.

The mirror shivered, then shattered—sending a wave of warm air across the clearing.

Ghurni stepped up to her pillar. The eye glowed, and before her appeared a maze—but it was invisible. She saw no walls, no signs, only shifting light on the ground.

"It's a maze of logic," she murmured. "But I have to feel it."

Using pebbles, the weight of her steps, and her instincts, Ghurni mapped an invisible pattern across the stone, careful not to trigger the glowing lines that occasionally flickered at the edge of her vision.

One wrong step would send her back.

One right one would lead her on.

After what felt like hours, Ghurni reached the center—and the maze vanished.

Her pillar pulsed gold.

Meghna approached the flame symbol. The pillar grew hot—but only in the mind. She could see flames licking around her, but there was no heat. Her test was to control her fear, not the fire.

She took a deep breath, remembered her parents' calm voices whenever she got scared, and reached into the illusionary fire.

Her hand passed through.

There was no burn—only light.

She pulled free a tiny glowing shard—crimson and radiant.

The final Heartstone.

The three girls stood side by side. Three trials passed. Three pillars glowing. The Heartstone floated above them—joining the other two already in their possession.

The magical book opened on its own. New lines appeared:

"The flame has been restored.

The guardians have awakened.

But shadows do not sleep."

Suddenly, the sky cracked open with a piercing scream.

Black clouds poured across the sky, and a massive shape rose from the far side of the forest.

The Shadow Guardian.

Twisted, winged, and born from darkness.

It was coming for them.

Chapter 27
The Shadow Guardian

The wind roared. The sky darkened, as if a lid had been slammed shut over the sun. Shadows writhed like living things along the edge of the crater. The girls stood together, holding hands, their backs to the glowing pillars. The final Heartstone hovered above them, pulsing with light—but it flickered, uncertain, as if sensing something ancient and wrong approaching. And then it came. From the dense mist at the far end of the clearing, a form emerged—tall, shrouded in swirling black fog, with eyes like glowing coals and wings that blotted out the sky. It didn't walk. It glided. Smooth. Silent. The Shadow Guardian had awakened.

Its voice thundered through their minds, not their ears. "You are not worthy. This temple does not belong to the weak. Surrender the Heartstones."

Ghurni tightened her grip on the compass. "We earned them. Solved every riddle. Faced every test."

The Shadow's voice deepened, echoing like distant thunder. "Power does not belong to children."

Kurchi stepped forward, her voice trembling but clear. "We didn't come for power. We came because the book chose us. Because this forgotten library wanted to be found."

The Shadow's smoky form flared, and with a terrifying screech, it lunged. The Heartstone reacted instantly, shielding the girls in a dome of light. The shadow-beast hissed, its form rippling, unable to breach the glowing barrier—but it circled them, tendrils of smoke lashing out like whips.

Meghna fumbled in her bag. “The magical book—it’s changing again!”

Pages turned wildly in the wind, then stopped—revealing a glowing circle. Symbols shimmered on the page: flame, voice, eye.

Ghurni read aloud. “The Guardian may not be defeated by force. It must be shown the truth it forgot.”

“What truth?” Kurchi asked.

The ground beneath them trembled. The pillars began to hum. Then, suddenly—Kurchi understood. She closed her eyes. She thought of the rooftop room. Of her father telling stories. Of rainy evenings and music classes and the first time she heard the Voicekeeper’s Guide hum back at her. She began to sing. It was not loud. It was not perfect. But it was full of memory. Of light. Of hope. As the melody floated across the crater, the Shadow Guardian froze. Its smoky form trembled. Fractures appeared in its wings. Its glow flickered, not with rage—but with recognition.

Meghna gasped. “It… it remembers.”

Meghna took the Heartstone from her satchel and raised it high. The flame leapt from it—not fire, but warmth, like the first sunlight after a storm. It pulsed outward in waves. She walked forward, step by step, into the darkness. The flame followed her, pushing the shadows back. “I believe in this,” she whispered. “In us. In this library. In everything we’ve found.” The Shadow screeched again—this time in confusion. Its shape melted and re-formed.

Ghurni ran to the compass. The needle spun madly, then stilled. A final riddle appeared in glowing letters above the Shadow's head:

"I once was guardian, fierce and bright,

Forgotten now, consumed by night.

Return to me my name, my spark—

And I will vanish with the dark."

Ghurni flipped through the book rapidly. On a nearly blank page, a name pulsed faintly—half-erased.

Aaravon.

"That's it!" she cried. "Its name is Aaravon!"

Kurchi sang the name into her melody.

Meghna held the Heartstone high.

And Ghurni spoke the final line of the riddle. There was silence. The crater lit with blinding white light. The Shadow Guardian screamed—not in anger, but relief. Its form burst apart in a thousand motes of silver, like ash on the wind. The clouds overhead split. Sunlight poured back into the clearing. The pillars dimmed. The ground stilled. And floating above the now-silent crater was a new book—thicker, older, bound in star-patterned leather. The cover read:

"The Library of Forgotten Guardians."

The girls stood breathless. Kurchi slowly reached for the book. It did not hum. It did not glow. It simply opened—revealing a single line: "You have restored what was lost. The Library remembers." From the forest, a breeze rustled the leaves. The compass snapped shut. The Heartstones merged into a single gem and nestled themselves into the new book's spine.

Ghurni exhaled. "We did it."

Kurchi nodded, stunned. "But what now?"

Meghna grinned. "We go home."

Later that evening, as dusk settled over the town, Kurchi's rooftop room felt warmer than ever. Her father placed a tray of samosas and hot milk in front of the girls, pretending not to notice how muddy and torn their clothes were. "You've had quite a day," he said, raising an eyebrow.

"Sort of," Kurchi replied with a grin.

Ghurni leaned back, watching the clouds turn pink. "We found the last Heartstone. Solved the Star Grave. Defeated a giant shadow thing. No big deal."

Meghna giggled. "Just another Tuesday."